the
   skirt
man

ALSO BY SHELLY REUBEN

Julian Solo

Origin & Cause

Spent Matches

Weeping

Tabula Rasa

shelly reuben

the skirt man

HARCOURT, INC.

Orlando   Austin   New York   San Diego   Toronto   London

OCo July 14
3+T
2400(1332)

www.HarcourtBooks.com

The photograph on page 247 is by Michael Reuben.

Library of Congress Cataloging-in-Publication Data
Reuben, Shelly.
The Skirt Man/Shelly Reuben.—1st ed.
p.   cm.
1. Eccentrics and eccentricities—Fiction. 2. Arson—Investigation—
Fiction. 3. New York (State)—Fiction. I. Title.
PS3568.E777S57   2006
813'.54—dc22   2006002580
ISBN-13: 978-0-15-101078-3   ISBN-10: 0-15-101078-1

Text set in Minion
Designed by Linda Lockowitz

Printed in the United States of America

First edition
K J I H G F E D C B A

the
skirt
man

chapter 1

THE SKIRT MAN.

In retrospect, it is amazing how many lives he touched.

Of course, "Skirt Man" wasn't his real name. His real name was Morgan Mason. But nobody ever called him that. And you can't blame them. What else would you call an old farmer who stuttered and drove his tractor into town a few times a week with his dog yapping along at his side wearing a skirt?

The man.

Not the dog.

My husband and I live on Willow Keep Road, which is less than two miles from the Skirt Man's farm. Small towns being what they are, though, Morgan Mason did his shopping in Killdeer, I did mine in Fawn Creek, and our twain had never met.

Not, at least, until...

Oh, so many things seemed to happen at once.

There was my job at the newspaper and my boss trying to retire. There was the benefit to raise funds for the town hall and our daughter, Merry, coming home to dance. There were those adorable Dillenbeck boys deciding to run the Skirt Man for mayor and then both of them falling in love with Merry at once. There was Creedmore Snowdon's campaign to turn Killdeer into Disneyland. And there was poor Rose Gimbel secretly playing Robin Hood; Lillian Roadigger's incomprehensible mood swings; Lewis Furth trying to start a range war; and that horrible Domingo Nogales Ramirez doing what he did to the old Hobby Hills Horse Farm.

And, of course, there was the murder.

The journalist in me wants to start at the beginning of all these events and proceed logically to the end. But the involved citizen in me who knew, liked, loved, or loathed so many of the participants can't figure out where the beginning is.

So, I'll just close my eyes, take a deep breath, try to pin the tail somewhere on this donkey, and hope that I don't stab myself in the eye.

chapter 2

I DON'T AS A RULE write books.

Actually, I don't *ever* write books, because it requires too much brainwork. I have a theory that people are born with either long brains or short brains. Long-brain types design ocean liners or write histories of the Great War. Short-brain types build rowboats or draft articles on skirmishes that occur outside the perimeter of significant events.

I have a short brain.

I write for a small-town newspaper because it permits me to mete out words in sentences instead of paragraphs. If I had my druthers, I would be dropping these few pages on the desk of Slim Cornfield, my editor in chief, right now, and happily proclaiming, "I'm done."

Instead, I herein reproduce Morgan Mason's obituary from the July 19 issue of the *County Courier and Gazette*. It was written by the Skirt Man's sister, Decidia Skirball, and was accompanied by a forty-five-year-old picture taken from the Killdeer High School yearbook. It is a photograph of a young man with short dark hair, a rectangular head, a pugnacious jaw, piercing eyes, a thin mouth, and no smile. Since Decidia was estranged from her brother, I assume it was the only photograph of him that she had.

MORGAN MASON
OF KILLDEER

Morgan Mason passed away on Saturday, July 16, at the age of 63. He is survived by his nephew, Andrew Mason, and Andrew's wife, Neverly Mason. Andrew is a gentleman farmer with property in Killdeer. Morgan Mason was a lifetime farmer and a recent candidate for mayor. Funeral services will be postponed. In lieu of flowers, expressions of sympathy may be made to the Killdeer Society for Historic Preservation. There will be no calling hours.

I have always loved to study obituaries, which, if you think about it, are histories of a perfect length for someone with an abbreviated attention span. Over the years, I have become reasonably good at reading between their lines. In the case of the Skirt Man, that was quite easy to do, because I was familiar with so many of the parties involved.

Morgan Mason's sister, you will note, is conspicuously absent from the list of survivors. Her son, Andrew, is not. Decidia was always ashamed of her brother and snubbed him. In private. In public. In life and in death. She used his obituary, however, to elevate the status of Andrew from local landowner, which he was, to "gentleman farmer," which he was not. And she did not she fail to mention that the Skirt Man was a candidate for mayor, a prestigious accomplishment even though he had nothing to do with his own candidacy and Decidia had vehemently opposed it.

Details about the life, accomplishments, and manner of death of Morgan Mason are glaringly omitted from this death notice. There is no explanation for the postponement of his funeral. And Decidia's requesting that donations be made in the Skirt Man's name to the Killdeer Society for Historic Preservation, an organization that detested him, is a downright sacrilege.

I got hold of a copy of the obituary before press time and was so appalled by it that I immediately called the Dillenbecks and asked Sonny and Moe if they wanted to write something about him for the *County Courier*'s front page. They contributed this:

Morgan Mason. Our Friend.
by Sonny Dillenbeck and Moses Dillenbeck

About six months ago, back in January, our father told us to drive to Mrs. Pinch's house and help her get her wedding ring out of the kitchen drain. The temperature that day was up over sixty degrees. After we finished with Mrs. Pinch, we were over on Route 39 on our way back to Dad's hardware store when this deer ran in front of our car and came pretty close to getting us killed. Snow was melting everywhere and the puddles were as big as lakes. After we swerved to avoid the deer, we got stuck on the shoulder of the road.

There wasn't much traffic that day. Well, actually, there wasn't any, and after about half an hour we were getting pretty antsy. That's when we saw this old Ford tractor coming our way. A few minutes later, Mr. Mason drove up.

We had never heard of him back then because we didn't grow up in the area and had only lived here a couple of years. If we had, though, we probably would have known that he was pretty much considered to be an oddball, that he was called the Skirt Man because he wore long, heavy skirts over his dirt-kicking boots, and that everyone made fun of him behind his back.

All we knew was that this weirdly dressed but otherwise regular-looking old guy who hardly said a word, and stuttered when he did talk, pulled us out of the mud, towed us behind the tractor to his house, and made us a couple of pretty good cups of tea while we waited for Dad to pick us up.

If we had normal parents, it probably would have ended right there, but our mom must have been hit on the head by an etiquette book when she was a kid, because enough is never enough for her. After our car was fixed, she made a batch of brownies and told us we had to go back to "that nice Mr. Mason" and thank him all over again.

Mom was right about one thing, because Mr. Mason really was a nice man.

The nicest.

And he became our friend.

We should explain right here that our grandfather, Rufus Dillenbeck, who everybody in town knew because he started the hardware store with our father, was killed by a bolt of lightning about a year ago. Ever since then, we kind of missed having him around. Mom said that we kept going back to see Mr. Mason because we needed a "cranky old man" in our lives to replace our grandpa, but honestly, Mr. Mason wasn't cranky at all. Just shy.

We could tell you a million stories about him, but everybody in town knows he was harmless, and you must have figured out by now that even though he wasn't very sociable, he had a sense of humor or he wouldn't have let us put him up for mayor, which we admit he never agreed to, but he also never told us that we had to withdraw his name, either.

Anyway, our tribute to Mr. Mason is that we are going to run for mayor as joint candidates in his honor, and we are going to implement the platform he didn't disagree with. We would also like to tell you what we think about how he died, but Mrs. Bly says we can't or we'll get sued. So, along with this being a tribute to our friend, it is an an-

nouncement of our candidacy. Our platform is: Vote For
Us and Paint Your Shutters Purple for All We Care.
Respectfully submitted,
Sonny and Moses Dillenbeck

It is true that I wouldn't let the boys write a word of their
theory about how Morgan Mason died. When and where he
died, however, are matters of public record. Very, very public,
given the television footage, the newspaper stories, the investigators, both sane and insane, and the opinions of just about
every living soul in the state, some of which must have been
arrived at after consulting Ouija boards.

As to the sane investigations, they were conducted primarily by my husband, New York State Police Investigator
Sebastian Bly, and my brother, New York City Supervising
Fire Marshal Billy Nightingale. Billy, at that time, was spend-
ing his vacation with us in Fawn Creek.

Coincidentally, both were in the Killdeer High School at-
tending a benefit ballet performed by our daughter, Merry,
on the night that the Skirt Man died. Or, as the announce-
ment appeared on the stage bill:

THE KILLDEER TOWN HALL
AUDITORIUM RESTORATION COMMITTEE
IS PROUD TO PRESENT
NEW YORK CITY BALLERINA
Meredith Bly

chapter 3

CREEDMORE SNOWDON has been called many things by many
people. I know this because I have read most of the gossip
columns and have heard a few choice contributions from acquaintances or co-workers with whom he has had dealings in
the past. My favorites include: brilliant, sly, arrogant, artistic,
high-handed, haughty, peremptory, relentless, insightful,
and effete. Based on what I have seen of him personally, I
would have to say that if you threw out anything in that list
that sounded remotely complimentary and kept the rest, it
would pretty much ring true.

I have also learned a bit from official biographers and
unofficial muckrakers about how Creedmore got from there
(childhood) to here (self-righteous adulthood). According
to these sources, he went to New York University, where he
took film courses and met Decidia Skirball. She had recently
moved to Manhattan from Killdeer and was still brushing
the hayseeds out of her hair. They took an instantaneous liking to each other. He gave Decidia away at her wedding. He

was her confidant during her marriage. He was the godfather to her son Andrew. They became lifelong friends.

Although Creedmore's overriding ambition was to become a television producer, he took a profitable detour during the several years that he interviewed the rich and famous for *Town & Country* and *Vanity Fair* magazines. This was followed by a stint on a television show called *Star Speak* where, for fifteen years, he talked to and about celebrities. Finally, after finishing what he referred to as his "apprenticeship with lower life forms," he went on to produce a television series called *Heaven and Earth*, which he conceived, wrote, directed, and hosted.

From the very first episode, *Heaven and Earth* was wildly successful and it skyrocketed Creedmore to fortune and fame.

The program, which you can see every Sunday evening at eight, sensationalizes the unexplained and dramatizes phenomena that science has never listed in its table of contents. This includes UFOs, after-death experiences, automatic writing, ESP, telekinesis, exorcisms, mind reading, and reincarnation.

Before each episode, Creedmore Snowdon (a name of dubious ancestry, since he was born of Lithuanian parents who lived on Staten Island) is seen wearing his trademark white linen suit and paisley bow tie. He is reclining, as if on an invisible sofa, in topless and bottomless space. His longish silver hair is surrounded by a halo-like circle of light, and the expression on his pale ageless and sexless face is meditative and intense. A few gauzy clouds drift by. Haunting music creates an eerie atmosphere, and Creedmore begins to talk. With a phony British accent and in a voice that just misses being resonant, he says: "There are more things in heaven and earth than are dreamed of in our poor philosophies, my friends." By the time he has finished misquoting Shakespeare, Creedmore is completely enveloped by clouds, and the words "Heaven and Earth" are illuminated in ghostly lettering across the screen.

Although this show is patently ridiculous and could only be taken seriously by someone who might subscribe to *Paranormal Housekeeping* magazine, it is extremely entertaining to watch people getting stupid over bent spoons and trick photography. The program had been on for over a decade when, to many people's eventual dismay, its creator, producer, and director decided to move to our very own Chenango County and take up residence in Killdeer.

The blame for Creedmore doing this can be laid directly at Decidia Skirball's expensively clad feet.

After forty-five years of living in Manhattan and pretending that she was not a farmer's daughter, Decidia became a widow after her successful Wall Street banker husband died. Left alone for the first time in her adult life, she was suddenly inspired to come "home." Decidia bought and renovated the Cranford place on Magnolia Drive, a beautiful old Victorian on almost two acres of land, with wide porches, gingerbread trim, and a lushly landscaped pond inhabited by belligerent swans. Once she had settled in, she sent change-of-address cards to all of her society friends, invited Creedmore for a visit, and reinvented herself as a doyenne of the countryside.

Decidia and Creedmore had never been lovers, but they shared a love of gossip that bound them closer than many people who have shared a bed. This may go a long way toward explaining why, less than four months after Decidia left New York City, Creedmore suddenly decided that Killdeer was the pleasant, quaint, and charming village he had been looking for his entire life, and that he couldn't live another moment without acquiring a weekend retreat—a decision that delighted Decidia to no end and prompted her to contact her favorite real estate agent.

Creedmore had looked at only three houses before he was shown a well-maintained Federal less than five minutes from Decidia's opulent Victorian. He bought it for cash.

Within six weeks of moving to Killdeer, he was already considering another move. This one into politics. Creedmore's television series was doing well; he was in perfect health; and life was good. But he craved a new challenge. A challenge, he told Decidia, that would not only invigorate him, but also restore and revitalize "their" little town.

Killdeer, he was certain, needed him; and it needed him more than he needed it.

And so, in the vacuum created by events at the Hobby Hills Horse Farm, which I will explain later, he decided to run for mayor, vowing that he would make Killdeer as attractive, pristine, and popular as Cooperstown or Skaneateles. It would be the next (but not final) triumph in a life that had achieved everything that makes living rewarding and palatable.

Professional success and financial security?

He had already acquired both.

The only objective he had not yet attained was power.

Technically, the house that Creedmore Snowdon bought was located within the village limits, but it was actually two blocks north of Killdeer proper on Route 39. The Skirt Man's farm was also on Route 39. It was 5.4 miles from where Creedmore lived, a fact that became relevant considerably before the night of July 16.

A Saturday night.

The same Saturday as the benefit being held in the high

school auditorium. The benefit that starred Merry. Creed-more had been scheduled to emcee the festivities, and despite my aversion to the man, there was no question that his name on the playbill helped sell tickets. After all, everybody loves a celebrity, and ten dollars a seat is more than the locals are usually willing to pay.

Like it or not, our sold-out crowd had not come just to see my darling daughter dance.

By eight o'clock that night, we knew that the evening was going to be a huge success. But not because Creedmore had deigned to honor us with his presence since he ended up not getting there in time. About two hours before curtain, the benefit planners got an indignant telephone call from our celebrity complaining that his airplane was stuck—"Can you believe it? Stuck!"—on a JFK runway, and that if he was lucky, he "just *might* get to Killdeer before everybody in the audience has packed up their runny-nosed brats and gone home."

To fill the gap, one of the benefit's planners talked our town historian, Lillian Roadigger, into taking over the duties as host. At exactly eight thirty, all five feet one inch of the pretty public health nurse walked confidently on stage. Lillian, who prior to that evening had always seemed shy and self-effacing, apologized for Creedmore's absence and explained that he still might arrive early enough to greet people personally at the end of the show.

Then she treated us to a brief and fascinating history of the Killdeer Town Hall. She spoke about the magicians, singers, and fiddlers who had performed there, and the films that had been shown in the past, the very first of which was Lon Chaney's *Phantom of the Opera*.

"After the auditorium is refurbished," Lillian announced with a captivating gleam in her eye, "the restoration committee is scheduling a special showing of that very same silent movie, accompanied by the original organ that provided music for it over eighty years ago. So make sure you are all in good voice, because we expect you to boo the villains and cheer the heroes at the top of your lungs!"

Lillian then went on a bit (never too much as far as I'm concerned) about my daughter's success as a principal ballerina and introduced Meredith as the star of the evening.

The audience applauded enthusiastically, and Lillian left the stage, looking to all who knew her very much like a butterfly who, after fifty-seven years of evolution, had finally shrugged off her cocoon and kicked it contemptuously under the bed.

I will refrain from describing Merry's performance because I do not want to incur the wrath of the thousands of mothers out there with ugly and untalented daughters who look like toads. Instead, like the good reporter I am, I will merely state that during Act II, at 9:05, Creedmore Snowdon's plane landed at the Binghamton airport, after which he retrieved his car from the long-term parking lot and headed south along Route 39.

It was a brilliantly clear, moonlit summer night. Creedmore was driving fast and his temper had not improved; he was very conscious that by not getting to the auditorium on time he would be missing an opportunity to remind the people of Killdeer that he was running for mayor. Despite his desire to arrive before the end of the benefit, however, his foot eased off the gas pedal as he approached the Skirt Man's farm.

To most of the people in Killdeer, Morgan Mason was no more offensive than a bad haircut or a corny joke. Creedmore Snowdon, however, was not "most people." He saw no humor in the old farmer's stocky frame, pale green eyes, massive chest, or long drab skirts. And he was no more willing to tolerate Morgan Mason than he would a case of shingles or strep throat.

Nor, whenever he drove past the Skirt Man's house, did Creedmore see the dark green shutters, white clapboard siding, colorful flowerbeds, or acres of neatly cultivated crops.

All he saw, all he *ever* saw, was a huge, dark gray satellite dish, as irritating to him as a wrinkled shirt or a smudge of mustard on the lapel of his white linen suit.

Creedmore continued to decelerate as he drew closer to the farm because it gave him an intoxicating, stomach-churning, and wound-salting pleasure to draw out, nurture, and cultivate his hatred. He rounded a slight curve in the road. His headlights dipped for an instant and then rose to illuminate the gargantuan satellite dish.

Fifty miles an hour.

Forty-five miles an hour.

Thirty miles an hour.

His foot retreated from the gas pedal.

As Creedmore later related to anyone willing to listen to his dramatic reenactment, he felt, for a second, as if he had been transported back to the prologue of his own television show. Misty clouds drifted across his line of vision and moonlight reflected eerily in the dark windows of the Skirt Man's house. All around him, there was a sense of the surreal.

But this was not television, and he was not looking at clouds.

It was smoke.

And it was coming from inside the Skirt Man's house.

Creedmore Snowdon swerved into Morgan Mason's driveway, his brakes screeching as he negotiated the turn. He leaped out of the car, ran up the shallow porch steps, and pushed on the door.

It flew open.

A blast of hot air hit him in the face, stinging his eyes and driving him back along the porch.

"Morgan," he shouted. "Mr. Mason?"

There was no answer.

He called out again, inching forward into the heat and the haze.

Then, slowly, tentatively, as though each foot were being placed on stepping-stones across the burbling turmoil of a swamp, he maneuvered himself into the house.

chapter 4

BY THE TIME my daughter was eighteen years old, she was already touring with the Manhattan Delacourte Ballet Theater and had danced in lead roles in Philadelphia, Chicago, New Orleans, San Francisco, Los Angeles, and Dallas. And, pardon me if I brag, just a few weeks before the benefit for the Killdeer Town Hall, Merry had come back from a tour that included London, Paris, Milan, and Madrid.

So, even though it was fun for her to perform in a high school auditorium not far from where she grew up, it was not exactly the high point in her career.

That Merry was dancing in Killdeer at all was actually a bit of a fluke. Her former teacher, Arabella McKenzie, who'd had a brief but torrid love affair with my brother, Billy, had originally agreed to donate her own time and talent, but at the last minute had been invited to appear as guest artist in a new incarnation of the old Ballets Russes de Monte Carlo. As a dancer, this was an offer that Arabella felt she could not afford to refuse. Which left the town hall benefit in a bit of a bind.

Arabella knew that Merry would be on summer break, so

she asked her former student if she could or would—"Please, dear. It would mean so much to me"—take over the job. She offered Merry the use of any or all of her students, costumes, sets, the dancers from her Lyric Ballet Company, and even (she was either desperate or joking) her bicycle, jewelry, goldfish, cell phone, and herbal shampoo.

Merry agreed.

She selected her own program and decided to present abbreviated versions of two of Arabella's ballets—sweet things based on O. Henry stories. To help with sets, props, and lighting, Merry was given permission by the head of the drama department at Killdeer High School to appeal personally to the junior and senior classes and ask for volunteers.

At the time these events occurred, Merry was all of nineteen years old—not exactly an age anyone would categorize as "older woman." That, however, is exactly what she seemed to be to Sonny and Moses Dillenbeck when they saw her for the first time. She was standing at the head of their class, less than fifteen feet away. She was a famous (well, to them if not yet the world) ballerina, wearing a frothy, pastel summer dress and looking every bit as substantial as a sigh. She was an exquisite, fairylike creature, and she was asking *them* (neither could believe their ears) for *their* help.

Their hearts flopped out of their chests and dropped like water balloons to the floor.

It was love at first sight.

The clincher for Sonny was Merry's pale porcelain complexion, long swan neck, and the fragile symmetry of her bones.

For Moe, it was her huge brown eyes, her delicately chiseled nose, and the uninhibited tangle of her wild red hair.

They trampled the other boys out of the way, climbed over six desks, and literally fell at her feet.

Sonny Dillenbeck was seventeen years old and he was white, as in Caucasian. Moe was a month older; he was six feet three inches tall, slim, muscular, and black, as in Negro. When they were still toddlers, Moe's father, Boyd, fell in love with Sonny's mother, Netty. They got married, adopted each other's children, marveled that the boys were so similar in outlook and disposition, and began to call them psychic twins.

Sonny had dark blond hair, gold-flecked hazel eyes, and a strong jaw. He also had a set of really adorable dimples that popped out—or was it in?—when he smiled, and he smiled often because he was a happy guy. Sonny had gravitated toward the theater because he intended to be an actor when he grew up. So, aside from his ulterior motive of wanting to breathe the same air that Merry did, it was natural that he would respond to her appeal.

Moe's grandfather, Rufus, the one who was hit by a bolt of lightning, had spent thirty years in the New York City Fire Department before he opened the hardware store in Killdeer. Moe's childhood had been filled with stories of alarms going off in the middle of the night, daring and dangerous search-and-rescue operations, and the brotherhood of firemen. By the time he was six years old, Moe knew that, like his grandpa, he was going to be a fireman, too.

Moe had a huge nose, tousled black hair, a dopey smile, gargantuan feet, and beautiful hands. He never would have wanted to have anything to do with the stage, except that he had taken one look at Merry and, like Sonny, his heart had done a belly flop to the floor.

That Merry got a big kick out of being an adored "older woman" goes without saying. After all, she *is* my daughter. On top of that, Sonny and Moe's antics when they weren't moving sets, arranging props, or operating spotlights made her laugh so hard that, twice, she almost fell out of her chair.

Those of you who don't know Merry won't appreciate how unusual this was, as Meredith Bly, although she *does* have a sense of humor, has never been a slap-her-thigh and yuk-it-up kind of a girl. Merry, in fact, is well known for her composure, her poise, her elegance, and her reserve.

Well, Sonny and Moe made short shrift of that.

Observing the progression of this three-sided love affair, Sebastian developed the theory that Sonny and Moe weren't really in love with Meredith at all; they were just hopelessly addicted to making her laugh.

Two goofy seventeen-year-olds who even *think* that they are in love were a perfect antidote to the unrelenting discipline and fanatical purposefulness of ballet.

Sonny asked Merry if she would marry him after he grew up and became a famous movie star.

She laughed.

Moe asked Merry to become *his* wife instead and be the mother to his future children. All seven of them.

She spilled coffee down the front of her leotard.

Sonny asked her to marry Moe.

Moe asked her to marry Sonny.

They followed her around like knights in shining armor on sick leave from common sense. When Merry rehearsed, they sat in the first row of the auditorium and gazed up at her with lovesick eyes. Sonny would elbow Moe in the ribs and say, "Isn't she great?" Moe would elbow Sonny in the ribs and say, "That's my future wife."

Their pride and joy in her performance on the night of the benefit would probably have caused them to burst blood vessels if they hadn't found an outlet for their feelings. They could not afford the jewels, flowers, and champagne that typical Stage-Door Johnnies showered on the object of their affection. But they did manage to present Merry with something meaningful. Something memorable. Something that nobody else in the whole world would ever have thought to give her.

Their means of acquiring their objective was not entirely judicious, but once it had been obtained, they adorned it in a way they thought appropriate, tucked it under a blanket in a wicker basket, and after Merry had finished a dazzling performance to a standing ovation, brought it to her backstage.

Their idea of an appropriate tribute was a four-week-old pygmy goat.

Not a stuffed toy pygmy goat.

The real thing. Bleating. Breathing.

Alive.

There are two reasons why I have gone on here at such length about Sonny and Moe's infatuation with our daughter. One is that I like to write about Merry and would manufacture excuses to do so even if I did not have real reasons. Two is that, because they were in the launch position to give her a goat, the boys were less than four feet away from us when Gerry Gilbert, assistant chief of the Killdeer Volunteer Fire Department—and my manicurist's husband—clattered anxiously up the backstage stairs. Two strides behind Gerry was a huffing, puffing Creedmore Snowdon, our absentee host of the evening. His usually perfectly combed hair was tousled, his white linen suit was dirty, and his soft face was flushed with excitement, fear, and nerves. There was a thin coating of what looked like gray dust on his shoes, and his paisley bow tie was dangling at an angle that would not have been allowed under any Adam's apple in *Gentleman's Quarterly.*

"Sebastian," Gerry said gruffly, one of his calloused truck-driver hands grabbing for my husband's arm. "We got a problem."

Sebastian gave Merry a kiss and a hug, said, "Excuse me," and moved over to join the assistant chief.

I followed.

So did my brother, Billy Nightingale.

So did Merry, Sonny Dillenbeck, Moses Dillenbeck, and the goat.

Since Sebastian was used to us, and since he hadn't noticed Sonny and Moe, he said, "Yeah, Gerry?" as if none of us were there. Killdeer's assistant fire chief, who was also accustomed to Bly family togetherness, ignored us as well.

He said, "Mr. Snowdon here just came from old Morgan Mason's house. He saw smoke when he was driving by, and stopped. He says he was able to get inside as far as the living room, but that the Skirt Man was already dead."

Creedmore Snowdon, who had been scowling impatiently during the assistant chief's recital, could hold it in no longer and burst out, "I tried to call 911." His voice was both aggressive and whiny at the same time. "I couldn't get a signal on my cell phone. It doesn't—"

Gerry cut him off. "Most of our guys were in the audience just now, Sebastian. Ralph went over to sound the alarm. I told the chief I'd join them at the firehouse in—"

The loud and melancholy wail of a siren broke off his explanation.

"There it is," Gerry Gilbert said unnecessarily.

Sebastian turned to Creedmore.

"Tell me about the fire."

Creedmore's nostrils flared and the expression on his face was—well, the only word that comes to mind is haughty.

"I can add nothing to what has already been said."

"Are you sure Mr. Mason is dead?"

"One would hardly mistake what I observed as . . . as . . . as . . ."

And he stopped.

His skin turned white, beads of sweat literally popped

out on his forehead, and I could see his stomach begin to heave.

Reality had caught up with the television producer.

Sebastian and Billy exchanged a glance.

They moved to one side, leaving an unobstructed path to the backstage bathroom. Creedmore stumbled past them, one hand clasped over his mouth.

Sebastian turned to Billy.

My brother and my husband have what they like to call a "reciprocal forensic relationship," which is a fancy way of saying that they enjoy playing cops and robbers on each other's turf. When we stay at our apartment in Manhattan, Sebastian goes along in Billy's squad car to fire scenes; when Billy visits us in Fawn Creek, he rides shotgun during Sebastian's tour of duty.

Because Billy is a supervising fire marshal with the New York City Fire Department and an expert at investigating fires, he has also, over the years, helped the state police with some origin-and-cause investigations.

"You coming?" Sebastian asked Billy.

"Clear it with your supervisor and I'll get my camera bag," Billy answered.

They had taken less than two steps toward the stage-door exit when a rustle of feet and a clumsy repositioning of knees, shoulders, and legs stopped them. Sonny Dillenbeck, or maybe it was Moe, crashed into Sebastian from behind.

"Excuse me, Mr. State Trooper. With all due respect, wait up a second, sir."

Sebastian stopped.

He turned and glared. Despite his irregular features, my husband is a very affable-looking man. He has gorgeous thick black hair and dark eyes more inclined to twinkle than to brood. But he is large, and when he wants to, he can exude an air of official state police authority.

"Make it quick," he said.

"Yes, sir," Moe saluted.

"We knew him," Sonny blurted out, elbowing his brother out of the way.

"Yeah," Moe's elephant-sized foot descended on Sonny's toe. "We knew him really well."

"Who?"

"Mr. Mason."

"We go to his house all the time."

"He is . . . was our friend," Moe or Sonny said mournfully.

"We want to help."

Sebastian looked at Billy, who was staring down at the wicker basket Moe was clutching in his arms. A blanket covered something inside that appeared to be moving. Billy reached over and flipped up an edge of the blanket. The sweet face of a small animal stared back. It had big, trusting, brown eyes and cheerful ears surrounded by soft tufts of white fur. There was an enormous pink bow tied around its neck

Billy raised an eyebrow.

"It's a pygmy goat," Sonny said.

"For Merry," Moe added. He thrust the basket into my arms—why me, for heaven's sake? The goat was supposed to be for Merry—and said to Sebastian, "Well?"

Sebastian studied the boys for a few seconds.

"Okay," he said. "Take your own car and don't get in my way."

Then he and Billy strode down the hall.

chapter 5

IF BILLY NIGHTINGALE had written a report on the fire in the Skirt Man's house, it would have started out like this:

OWNERSHIP AND OCCUPANCY

The fire under investigation occurred in a residence owned by Morgan Mason, age 63, who was the sole occupant of the house.

It is located on 235 acres of land. There is a small natural lake on the property about 1,000 feet southwest of the driveway. It is not visible from the house. Additional structures on the property include a barn, a silo, an outhouse (not in use), and an old chicken coop that has been converted into an equipment shed. There is a doghouse between the porch and the driveway but no dog in evidence.

The occupancy itself is a one-story dwelling of wood-frame construction, approximately 30 feet by

```
33 feet, on a concrete slab. It has clapboard sid-
ing, an asbestos shingle roof, an oil-heat furnace,
and 220 overhead electrical wiring reduced to 110
volts.

Access to the residence is attained through a door
on a small porch that faces the driveway. This ex-
terior door opens into a small, enclosed hall with
clothes hooks and a storage bin, and from there into
a center hall that divides the house approximately
in half. To the left of the entrance hall is the liv-
ing room, which was the area of origin of the fire.
```

Sebastian sped the 5.4 miles from the village of Killdeer, past the entrance to Hobby Hills—our friendly, neighborhood drug haven—and parked on the shoulder of the road. He backed up so that his headlights were shining on the door to Morgan Mason's house, and he watched as the Dillenbeck boys parked about fifty feet away. Then he took a flashlight out of his glove compartment, gave it to Billy, reached under the seat for another flashlight, and strode to where Sonny and Moe were still seated in the front seat of their car. He leaned down to the window and said, "Don't even think of following us."

Billy grabbed his camera bag. Before he and Sebastian had finished crossing the road, they saw the red jeep of Tom Mansfield, chief of the Killdeer Volunteer Fire Department, skidding into the Skirt Man's driveway. Fifteen seconds later, it was followed by the department's Pierce Pumper and its 2,000-gallon tanker.

Almost immediately, volunteer firefighters in turnout gear piled out of the trucks and began a rugged ballet of men and machines. Sebastian and Billy stood off to the side as

Chief Mansfield ordered Frank Garfield and Ralph DeSotto into the house. Mel Lispenard went around the back, and the Hardcastle brothers, Jay and Simon, climbed up on the roof. Within minutes, though, all activity ceased. The men returned to the driveway and began to stow their equipment and take up their hoses.

Sebastian approached the chief.

"Tom," he said. "This is Bill Nightingale. He's going to help us with the cause and origin of this fire. Billy, this is Chief Mansfield. Tom owns the Chrysler dealership in town."

Tom Mansfield nodded pleasantly to Billy. "You live here?"

"I visit," Billy said. "The ugly guy who introduced us is my brother-in-law."

The chief grinned. "Yeah. He is pretty ugly."

"Can you keep the overhaul to a minimum, Chief?" Billy asked.

"Don't need to do any overhauling. The fire's out. Been out for a while. No hotspots. No pockets of flame. Nada."

"Then I don't have to ask you to use a fog nozzle either."

"No, you don't. Why? You suspect something fishy?"

Billy shrugged. "You know. Guys like me are obsessed with preserving evidence."

Nobody had to ask evidence of what.

On the numerous occasions when I have hounded Billy to divulge every last detail about one fire case or another, he has explained to me (and Sebastian) that since there is no way of knowing where or how a fire started until *after* an investigation has already been conducted, all fire scenes, even the most innocent-seeming ones, have to be treated as potential crime scenes whether they are or not.

"I left it the way I found it," Chief Mansfield said to Billy. "If there's any evidence in there, you're welcome to it." Then he added to Sebastian, "Nothing more to do here."

"Thanks, Tom."

The chief jutted his head toward the Skirt Man's house.
"Sad," he said.

"Did you know him?" Billy asked.

"Not to talk to. But..." He paused for a moment, as
though trying to find the right words. "You didn't have to
know the Skirt Man to know him, if you get my drift. Him
and his dogs. Driving into town every few days on that tractor. Different dog every fifteen years or so, but not so as you'd
notice. He wasn't a sociable man. He'd nod politely enough if
you said hello. But he didn't talk. Maybe he was embarrassed
because he stuttered. If that television guy hadn't seen smoke,
could have been days, maybe weeks, before anyone found
him. I don't think he had a friend in the world. Still, I'll miss
him. A lot of people around here will. Like I said, it's sad. The
Skirt Man was like...like a fixture."

Chief Mansfield shook his head, as if to shake off his
mood.

"Well, I'll be going now, Sebastian. The scene's all yours.
The Chenango County Arson/Fire Task Force will be along
presently, and I'll put in a call to the county coroner and have
him see to the body."

The chief gave Sebastian a two-fingered salute, got in his
car, and drove away, with the Killdeer Fire Department appa-
ratus pulling out of the driveway right behind him.

Billy watched the trucks disappear down the road. Then
he started to walk toward the back of the house.

"Where are you going?" Sebastian asked, flicking on his
flashlight.

"I want to do a quick check of the perimeter."

Most fire investigators do that. The good ones, at least.
They circle the outside of the structure that burned to get an
overall picture of where fire may have broken through, and if

any incendiary devices, gas cans, or incriminating artifacts had been left behind. They check for smoke or fire damage to the exterior and anything else that will add to their store of knowledge before they go inside.

Billy was still circling the house and Sebastian had just started up the porch steps when he felt a tap on his left shoulder.

Moses Dillenbeck, a somber expression on his youthful face, said, "Excuse me, sir."

Sebastian turned. He did not look warm and fuzzy.

"I thought I told you boys to stay in the—"

He felt a tap on his right shoulder.

"We can't find Buddy," Sonny said.

Sebastian took a deep, steadying breath. He is very, very strict about protocol at a crime scene.

"Who," he said sternly, "is Buddy?"

"Mr. Mason's dog," both boys said at once.

"Maybe Buddy's off chasing a rabbit."

"He doesn't chase rabbits. He doesn't chase anything. He's old."

"So maybe he died."

"He was alive yesterday," Sonny said.

"Yeah," Moe agreed. "He barked at us when we drove past. A real enthusiastic bark. Dead dogs don't bark that loud."

Billy walked over to join Sebastian on the porch.

"Look, boys," he said soothingly. "We know you're concerned about your friend, and we admire you for it. Good friends make good men, and you two were good friends of Mr. . . . Mr. . . ."

"Jeeesh," Moe said disgustedly. "You could at least learn his name."

"Which is . . . ?"

"Morgan Mason."

"Mr. Mason. I'll remember it. That's my part of the deal. Your part is that you've got to give us a little room here to do our jobs."

"Yeah," Sebastian said with no attempt at sounding conciliatory. "Wait for us in your car. We'll let you know if we need your help."

Sonny rolled his eyes at Moe. Moe looked at his brother and nodded. They turned and started to walk away. But not back toward their car.

"Hey," Sebastian shouted. "Where do you think you're going?"

Moe swiveled his head briefly.

"To find Buddy."

They continued to walk past the house.

Just as they were about to disappear around the corner of the barn, Sonny called out, "Don't worry, Mr. State Trooper, sir. We won't touch anything."

BILLY NIGHTINGALE grew up on a ranch in Elks Mountain, Wyoming.

So did I.

When he was still a teenager, we had a fire in our barn, and for longer than any of us want to remember, my brother was suspected of having set that fire. My father never thought Billy was guilty, but when the insurance company refused to pay the claim and the ranch hands started to look at Billy funny, he decided it was time to call in his old war buddy, Delmore O'Shaughnessy, who had become a deputy chief fire marshal in New York City.

As a favor to my father, O'Shaughnessy flew to Wyoming to investigate the fire in our barn. Billy took to the veteran fire marshal immediately and followed him through every step of the investigation. During that intense hour or two, O'Shaughnessy exposed my brother to the rudiments of fire analysis and showed him how to make sense of the apparently senseless aftereffects of a fire.

Two things happened as a result of their time together.

One: Chief O'Shaughnessy proved that Billy was not an arsonist and that the fire in the barn had been accidental.

Two: My brother decided to become a fire marshal when he grew up.

Being the oldest, I was the first of us to reverse Horace Greeley's historic mandate and went east instead of west. I had a passionate urge (even then I manifested short-brain tendencies) to be an extremely well-educated dilettante, a goal I believe I can claim to have achieved.

I went to college, graduated, and got a job at an art gallery in Manhattan. Billy, in short order, followed me to the city, graduated from the John Jay College of Criminal Justice, became a fireman, became a fire marshal, and had been a supervising fire marshal for eight years when the fire broke out in the Skirt Man's house.

Although Billy and I are similar in that we have the same temperament, the same outlook on life, and, like the Dillenbeck boys, can often communicate without saying a word, we are dissimilar in that we not only look as if we came from different wombs, we look like we came from different planets.

I have amber eyes and a small, heart-shaped face with no particular attribute that would get me installed in the Guinness Book of Goddesses. But at least all of my features are arranged around my nose in a not-unpleasant manner, and I have the normal complement of eyes, ears, fingers, and toes. My hair is short and brown. I have worn it in a pixie haircut since I gave my first engagement ring back to the first boy who proposed to me. Actually, it was his grandfather's Green Hornet decoder ring.

I am not very tall. Some heartless souls might even call me "short" as I only come up to the bottom of my husband's chin. But I have trained Sebastian to refer to me as a "pocket Venus," and that seems to work for both of us.

My devotion to Sebastian, by the way, is the only area of my life where I do *not* exhibit short-brain tendencies. My strong, sweet, lovable state police officer of a husband, who has, more or less, managed to extricate me from the Isle of Manhattan and domicile me in Fawn Creek, is a commitment for life. I am equally devoted to my daughter, my parents, my brother, and our dog, Murdock.

Speaking of my brother, Billy is much better looking than Sebastian and much taller than I. He comes from the Land of Blond, and even though he is in his early forties, his hair is still the color of sunshine and his eyes are still as blue as a Wyoming summer sky.

Whenever Billy is about to do something that requires intense concentration, his light eyes turn dark, dark blue, like the preamble to a storm. And when he opened the door to go inside the Skirt Man's house, it was as if someone had sneaked up on him with an eyedropper and surreptitiously added a drop of purple thunder to the azure iris of each eye.

BILLY UNSLUNG HIS camera bag and set it down on top of the radiator in the small enclosed entryway.

Sebastian flicked a wall switch.

"There's still electricity," he said.

They advanced into the center hall.

"Did you know this Mason guy?" Billy asked.

"I knew him when I was a kid. He scared me. He was a big guy. Big chest. Craggy, masculine face. He looked like a regular farmer except that he wore this really weird skirt and he stuttered. And like the chief said, he drove that old tractor into town for supplies and always had his dog with him."

"What was he like?"

Billy ran his hand against the wall to the left of the hallway, feeling for another light switch.

"The dog?"

"No. The man. But you can tell me about the dog. I'm not charging by the hour."

"They were all handsome animals. Usually German shepherds or Labs. Well-groomed and smart. If the Skirt Man told one of them to stay where it was when he went into the grocery store, you could throw a slab of beef in front of it, and it wouldn't budge."

"Sounds like Rin Tin Tin."

Billy moved to the other side of the opening to the living room and again felt along the wall for a switch.

"Do you think kids nowadays know who Rin Tin Tin is?"

"They probably think it's some kind of aluminum siding."

Sebastian directed the beam of his flashlight against the wall.

"Here's the switch," he said.

He reached out and flicked on the overhead light.

THE INVESTIGATORS at most fire scenes usually have a pretty good idea of where a fire started before they get to the area of origin. Often they'll just stick their heads inside the fire room to confirm their supposition and then go on to evaluate and document where the fire did *not* start.

A big part of fire analysis is elimination.

If an investigator says that the fire started in a defective electrical extension cord hooked up to the Christmas tree lights, he jolly well better make sure he can prove that it wasn't really caused by an unattended candle or a financially strapped homeowner who had rigged a timing device so that he could be out drinking martinis with his parish priest while his house burns down.

Similarly, if arson is suspected, the fire investigator will often take his "elimination photographs" during his preliminary go-around, before he does his comprehensive investigation of the area where he thinks the fire was set. Then, at a later date, when the defense attorney challenges his intelligence, integrity, and the legitimacy of his firstborn child, he will be able to prove on the witness stand that he did, indeed, examine and eliminate every possible alternative natural and accidental cause of the fire.

And so, camera in hand . . .

Utility room. Click.

Laundry room. Click.

Circuit breaker panels. Click.

Furnace room. Click.

Coffeemaker, toaster, microwave oven, stove, refrigerator, popcorn maker, and electrical outlets: Click, click, click, click, click, click, and click.

That is the way fires are usually investigated: from the area of least burning to the area of most burning.

But the fire in the Skirt Man's house was different.

The instant Sebastian switched on the overhead light, he and Billy were drawn inexorably forward.

Unconscious of impetus and momentum.

Unconscious of their surroundings.

Their eyes riveted on the horrific spectacle at the far corner of the room.

chapter 6

IT WAS AFTER SIX O'CLOCK Sunday morning when Sebastian and Billy finally got home. Merry was bone weary from all of those grand jetés and had gone to bed, but I had made a fresh pot of coffee and curled up on the sofa with a book to wait for them.

Exhibiting almost Olympian synchronization, I fell asleep at exactly the same moment my book fell out of my hand and hit me on the nose.

Sebastian tried to tiptoe past me on his way to bed, but the sofa I had picked was virtually unsneakpastable.

"Oh, no you don't," I said when I heard the creak of a foot pressing on a floorboard.

So my husband came over and sat heavily at my side.

"I didn't want to wake you up."

"You didn't," I lied, rubbing the sleep out of my eyes. "Where's Billy?"

"In the kitchen. Looking for something to eat."

I got up.

"What are you most?" I asked. "Hungry or sleepy?"

"Both."

"Come on. Tell me everything that happened while I fiddle you up some vittles. And don't leave out a single syllable, or *I'll know!*"

SEBASTIAN AND BILLY had been in the living room of the Skirt Man's house for over half an hour when they heard footsteps outside on the porch.

Billy said to Sebastian, "Keep them out. I'll be done here in a few minutes."

The Dillenbeck boys were already inside the entry hall when Sebastian interjected himself between where they were and where they thought they were going. Both boys looked awful. Sonny's mouth was pinched, his eyes were lowered, and deep worry lines furrowed his brow. Moe's big gargoyle face, instead of manifesting its usual goofy grin, wore a mask of tragedy.

Sebastian herded them back outside and down the stairs.

"Trust me on this." His voice was quiet, but firm. "You do not want to see what's inside."

Sonny sagged against the porch railing. "We didn't want to see what we just saw out there, either." He jutted his head in the direction of the barn. "Poor Buddy."

"What happened to Buddy?"

A big, glistening tear started to slide down Moe's cheek; it disappeared into the corner of his mouth. Then he sniffed just like a little kid and said so softly it was really a whisper, "Buddy is dead."

Sonny added, his breathing becoming rapid and irregular. "Don't . . . don't . . . worry." He choked back a sob. "We . . .

we . . . didn't . . . tou . . . tou . . . touch anything." And he gave a pathetic little laugh. "Lo . . . look at me. I sound just li . . . li . . . like Mr. Mason."

He pushed himself away from the railing and dropped down to the porch step. Moe folded his gangling body next to him and put an arm around his brother's shoulder.

"Poor Mr. Mason," Sonny said.

"Poor Mr. Mason," Moe repeated.

Sebastian gave the boys a few minutes to recover from too many traumas in too short a time. Then he hunkered down opposite them.

"Later on you're going to show me where you found Buddy," he said, sounding as coaxingly mild as he used to when he would try to convince Merry to show him a new Girl Scout badge or a dance step that she had recently learned. "Now we're just going to talk. All right?"

Neither boy said anything, but Sebastian perceived the microscopic nods of two heads. He stood up and looked around for something to sit on. He saw a bucket a few feet away, flipped it over, positioned it opposite Sonny and Moe, and sat down.

"I'm going to level with you because you were Mr. Mason's friends, but I want your promise first that you won't repeat anything you hear or learn today."

He looked at Moe first. "What's your name, son?"

"Moses Dillenbeck. Moe. I won't say anything."

He shifted to the other boy.

"You?"

"Sonny Dillenbeck. Me either."

Sebastian continued to eye the boys steadily, making a connection that the boys weren't aware of. Then he went on in a more sympathetic tone. "Earlier you heard someone say that your friend was dead. I'm sorry I have to tell you that what you heard is true. His body is in the living room and it's been badly burned."

Moe looked down and began to pick unconsciously at a splinter of wood on the stair.

"My grandpa told us that being burned in a fire is the worst way to die."

Sebastian rubbed his jaw. "It would be painful," he said simply. "But we don't know yet if the fire killed Mr. Mason or if it was something else."

Both boys jerked up their heads at the same time.

"Do you mean—" Moe began.

But before he could finish the sentence, the front door opened, and Billy Nightingale walked out.

Billy grabbed a chair from the porch, held it over his head while he stepped around Sonny and Moe, and dropped it next to Sebastian's bucket. Then he sat astride the chair with his arms folded around the back.

Sebastian waited until Billy was settled and started over.

"You boys don't know who I am, but I recognized your names. My name is Sebastian Bly. I'm Meredith's father."

"You're Merry's dad?" Sonny gasped, his features animated with curiosity for the first time since he had found the body of the Skirt Man's dog. He gave Moe a brotherly poke. "That's Merry's father," he said, the way Jimmy Olsen might have said, "That's Superman!"

"Hey," Moe said. "Pleased to meet you. I'm going to marry your daughter some day."

"Yeah," Sonny added. "Me, too."

Sebastian grinned and pointed a finger at Billy.

"This is Merry's uncle. Supervising Fire Marshal Bill Nightingale with the New York City Division of Fire Investigation. He's helping us out today and he's armed and dangerous. If you want to marry my daughter, you'll have to get past him first."

"Yes, sir," Sonny said.

"Yes, *sir!*" Moe repeated.

Sebastian turned to Billy. "Got anything to add?"

Billy raised an eyebrow and shook his head.

"Okay. Like I was saying, I've got to ask you boys a few questions because we aren't sure how Mr. Mason died."

Sonny and Moe exchanged a glance.

"You think he was *murdered,*" Sonny said, his eyes wide with anticipation.

"We don't think anything yet."

"Yeah. Sure." Moe snorted. His fingers dislodged the splinter he had been working on and he began to scrape away at a strip of peeling paint. "What do you want to know?"

Sebastian took a small pad and a ballpoint pen out of his shirt pocket.

"How did you two come to know the Skirt...I mean Mr. Mason?"

"It's all right. We know everybody called him that." Sonny slumped back against the porch railing. "We met him last winter when..."

And, each taking a turn, Sonny and Moe related pretty much the same story that they wrote down later for me when I asked them to contribute to the *County Courier and Gazette.*

"How often did you see him?" Sebastian asked. "You must be pretty busy at school."

"I'm on the basketball team," Moe said. "Sonny's in the drama club. We both work after school at the hardware store."

"Except when I'm in rehearsals for a play."

"Or I'm at basketball practice or in a game."

"We work for our dad all day Saturday, too. That's when we used to visit Mr. Mason."

"You see, old lady Pinch was always dropping jewelry down her drain. Sometimes her cat would get stuck in a crawl space or she'd lock herself out of her car. Anyway, at least once a week she would get herself mixed up in some sort of a catastrophe—"

"I think she makes them up because she has a crush on Moe."

"—and Dad would tell us to drive out to her house and fix whatever she broke."

"Since we had to drive past Mr. Mason's house, we stopped in every week or so on our way home."

"How long did you stay?"

"Half an hour. An hour. Mom usually made something for us to bring to him. Coffee cake. Cookies. Banana bread."

"What did you talk about?"

"Stuff."

"What kinds of stuff?"

"All kinds."

"Can you be more specific?"

Sonny looked at Moe. Moe looked at Sonny.

Moe's nose twitched and his eyes inadvertently swiveled toward the house. "It's kind of hard to think because... because..."

Billy stood up.

"Right. Not a smell you can get used to. Follow me. There are a couple of tree stumps over by the road."

The moon was full, and delicate tendrils of a light breeze gave instant relief to the men and boys as they distanced themselves from the heavy atmosphere of death.

Sebastian and Billy sat on one stump.

Sonny and Moe sat on the other.

Sebastian gave his brother-in-law a silent nod.

"I have some questions about the house," Billy took over somberly. "You boys know what it looked like before the fire. I don't."

"We never saw the *whole* house," Moe explained. "Only the living room, the kitchen, and the bathroom."

"All right. What do you remember about the seating arrangements in the living room?"

Neither boy answered immediately. Both boys seemed to be concentrating.

Then Sonny said, "We used to sit on an ugly brown tweed sofa. Mr. Mason sat by the window."

"On what?"

"One of those big, stuffy old chairs. We've got one in our den. It used to belong to our grandpa, and Mom is always threatening to have it reupholstered, but Dad says that's grounds for a divorce. It's got claw feet like a lion, it's all saggy and lumpy, and it's perfect for when you want to pretend you're reading but all you really want to do is sleep."

"Yep," Moe nodded his head. "Mr. Mason's chair was just like that. Why? Is it important?"

Instead of answering the question, Billy asked, "Did your friend smoke?"

"Cigarettes?"

"Right."

"No."

"A pipe?"

"I never saw him smoke a pipe, either."

"Do you know if he drank?"

"You mean booze?"

"Hard liquor. Beer. Wine."

"He drank tea. He made us a pot of . . . what did he call it? Darling?"

"No. Darjeeling."

"Yeah. That's it. Every time we stopped in, that's what he made for us."

"Do you know if he took prescription drugs?"

"I saw some aspirin in his bathroom."

"Anything else?"

"Bromo Seltzer?"

"Do you know why he wore a skirt?"

"No," Moe said firmly.

"Absolutely not," Sonny agreed. "You don't ask a farmer who looks like he could crush you with his bare hands why he's wearing a skirt. Not if you want to live."

"Point taken," Billy agreed. "How about visitors?"

"What about them?"

"Did he have any?"

"Well, Mr. Mason wasn't exactly a social butterfly."

"He liked the two of you," Sebastian interjected.

Sonny grinned. His dimples gave an impish charm to his handsome face.

Moe slapped his knees and laughed.

"Hell, Mr. Bly. Or should I call you Officer Bly? Or—"

"Since we're marrying your daughter—"

"Dad?"

Sebastian tried to swallow a smile.

The boys went on. "Like we said, Mr. Mason wasn't very sociable, but we got under his defenses."

"Yeah. We made him laugh."

"When we try and when we're not talking to the father of our future wife—"

"Some people actually *like* us."

Billy ignored the banter. "Do you know if anyone else visited him—other than the two of you?"

"We never saw anyone, but once when we dropped by, he was outside cleaning beer cans out of his flower beds."

Sonny pointed to a colorful display of pansies, primroses, poppies, petunias, and nasturtiums just north of the driveway.

"Mr. Mason's eyes would get real small when he was mad, and that day they were as small as raisins."

"Who was he mad at?"

"The people from Hobby Hills," Moe turned to look at a spot about twelve hundred feet from where we were sitting, which had once been the entrance to the Hobby Hills Horse Farm. A dozen or so years ago, it had been purchased by a man from downstate named Domingo Nogales Ramirez.

"You mean Mr. Ramirez?" Sebastian asked.

"No."

"Who?"

"Kids from Hobby Hills. They would drift through the gate, drugged out of their minds, and pass out in Mr. Mason's yard."

"They'd leave junk all over the place. Food wrappers. Beer bottles."

"Syringes."

"Yeah. He even found one of those."

"We keep a close eye on Hobby Hills," Sebastian said. "I never heard that Mr. Mason made any complaints."

"He wasn't a complaining kind of guy."

"Do you know if he ever had a run-in with Ramirez?"

"The creepy guy who owns Hobby Hills?"

"That's right."

"A few days ago, Mr. Mason drove his tractor right through that front gate past a bunch of dopers and make-believe security guards."

"What happened?"

"Don't know. We asked Mr. Mason, and he said, 'We ha ... ha ... had wo ... wo ... words.' That's a direct quote."

"Did your friend 'have words' with anyone else?"

"Sure did," Moe laughed cynically. "You know that big television mucka mucka—Creedmore Snowdon?"

Sebastian nodded.

Billy said, "I don't know him. Tell me."

"Okay," Moe said. "It's like this. Me and my movie-star handsome brother—"

"That's me," Sonny piped in.

"—a couple of years ago, we used to live in this other town."

"New Bassett," Sonny said. "Our parents moved there after they got married."

"Yeah," Moe said. "Don't be fooled because we look alike—"

Even Billy had to laugh at this description, because the contrast was so great between Moe, with his cocoa skin, huge nose, big ears, and long limbs, and Sonny, with his handsome face, fair hair, pale complexion, and expressive hazel eyes.

"Even though we look so much alike"—Moe milked the moment—"we are the products of broken homes."

"My father," Sonny said, "took a hike over the horizon."

"My mother," Moe added, "disappeared into a religious cult."

"So we only had two parents left."

"The *preferred* parents," Moe emphasized.

"My mom met Moe's dad," Sonny continued. "They fell in love. And after this, that, and the other thing, we all landed up in New Bassett."

Billy looked at his watch.

"Relax," Sonny said. "We're almost there. Now, New Bassett was a great place to grow up in. Until two years ago."

"That," Moe said, and his tone grew solemn, "is when the whole town—"

"Including where we lived—"

"Got turned into a historic district."

"Listed in the National Register of Historic Places."

"Protected by a historic preservation zoning ordinance."

"Boys . . ." Billy said impatiently.

"This is important," Sonny said.

"Right. It all ties in to Mr. Mason."

Billy took a deep breath. "Okay."

"After the ordinance was passed—"

"And we know all about this stuff because our parents were fighting like crazy to stop it."

"—everything changed in New Bassett."

"All of a sudden, you couldn't put a hammock in your front yard."

"Your kids couldn't sell lemonade on the sidewalk in front of their house."

"You couldn't repair your own car in your driveway."

"You were only allowed to hang your wash on a clothesline in your backyard one day a week between 9:00 and 11:00 A.M."

"You couldn't have an antenna on your roof."

"And God would strike you dead if you put up a satellite dish."

"Your house had to be painted a certain color."

"If you wanted to add a room, put in storm windows, or build a railing around your porch, you had to ask for permission from the preservation police."

"Mom and Dad hated that," Sonny said, his voice indignant.

"So, we moved to Killdeer."

"And we love it here. Or, at least we did until—"

"I get it." Sebastian snapped his fingers. "The campaign for mayor."

"Well, I don't get it," Billy said, leaning forward on the stump.

"Creedmore Snowdon," Sebastian said. "You know. The TV guy."

"Pudgy-faced, middle-aged pretty boy who told us about the fire?"

Sebastian nodded. "He's running for mayor."

"Yeah," Sonny said, taking up the story. "On a platform to turn Killdeer into New Bassett."

"Historic preservation." Moe stuck out his tongue, and put a finger in his mouth. "Barf."

"How does this tie in with your friend?" Billy persisted.

"Creedmore Snowdon hated Mr. Mason because he wouldn't take down the satellite dish."

"How do you know this?"

"He told us."

"Morgan Mason told you?"

"Uh huh. He said that one day the TV guy came to the farm and said the dish was a blot on the countryside and an eyesore and that Mr. Mason had to get rid of it."

"Which is a joke," Sonny added. "Because it's about fifty feet behind the barn, and you can only see it when you come around the curve by the culvert on Route 39. So who cares if it's an eyesore?"

"It was Creedmore's attitude," Moe said, picking at a loose thread from a tear in his blue jeans. "If he had asked politely, Mr. Mason would have taken it down."

"But then," Sebastian pointed out reasonably, "he wouldn't be able to watch television."

Sonny shrugged. "No big deal. The satellite dish was never hooked up to anything because Mr. Mason didn't have a TV."

"Then why—"

"Some farmer up the road sold his farm a few years back, and he asked Mr. Mason if he could leave the dish here until he bought a new place."

"But he died before he could pick it up."

"So Mr. Mason left it where it was and forgot about it until Creedmore Snowdon told him to take it down." Moe yanked at the thread, let it flutter for a second in the breeze, and then watched it drift to the ground. "You didn't *tell* Mr. Mason what to do."

"When we found out about the satellite dish," Sonny said, his voice a little shaky with emotion, "it sort of created a bond."

"That's why we became such good friends."

"And why he let us put in his name to run against Snowdon for mayor."

"It started out as a joke."

"But when Mr. Mason didn't tell us to stop, it got serious."

"Of course, he wouldn't have been able to make any speeches."

"It took him ten minutes just to say 'He...he...he... hello.'"

"So we were going to make the speeches for him."

"But now he's dead," Sonny said and sighed. Then both he and Moe stopped talking with such finality that it was as if they would never again have another word to say.

Sebastian and Billy were also silent for a few minutes. Finally Sebastian muttered, "Creedmore Snowdon hated Morgan Mason. He 'had words' with Domingo Nogales Ramirez at Hobby Hills. Was he on anyone else's hit list?"

Moe bit his lip pensively. "Well, his sister wasn't exactly a fan."

"How do you know that?"

"She's Snowdon's campaign manager. And she's got a son with about seventy-five acres of land half a mile up the road."

"Tell me more about the son."

"He tried to take over Mr. Mason's farm. Not buy it. Take it. As if he had the right."

"Anyone else?"

"Lewis Furth."

Sebastian frowned. "Half the countryside is pissed off at Lewis Furth. What did he do to your friend?"

"Mr. Mason's property ends at the tree line and Lewis Furth's farm is the next one over. Furth kept cutting holes in Mr. Mason's fence so that his cows could come through. Mr. Mason kept driving them back out and fixing the fence."

"Then Crazy Lewis started to move Mr. Mason's surveyor stakes so that it looked like he had more land and Mr. Mason had less. It got to be a range war."

"A range war," Billy repeated thoughtfully. "Anyone else mad at your friend? Disgruntled fertilizer salesmen? Turkey hunters? Cattle rustlers?"

Sonny looked at Moe.

Moe looked at Sonny.

They both shook their heads.

Billy stood up and took a deep breath.

"Okay," he said. "Let's go find that dog."

chapter 7

"WHAT ABOUT BUDDY?" I asked the kitchen at large, knowing that whoever didn't have a mouthful would answer first.

"Head bashed in." Billy leaned wearily against the back of his chair. "The boys found him under some branches behind the barn."

Sebastian started to reach for a muffin but his hand fell back against the table as if the effort had been too great. "The body wasn't hidden very well," he said. "Just dumped there. After the forensic unit arrived, I assigned a trooper to take Buddy to Cornell University. The dog is the reason it took us so long to get home."

I sliced the muffin in quarters, picked up one of them, and popped it into Sebastian's mouth. He would have to chew it himself.

"What about the Skirt Man?" I asked, knowing that Sebastian wanted the meticulous head pathologist at Binghamton General Hospital to do the autopsy.

"What about him?" My brother sleepily held out his cup. I refilled it and sat down.

the skirt man   49

"Didn't Aristotle Papas come to the fire scene?"

"He never comes to fire scenes. The County Arson/Fire Task Force came."

"What did they think?"

"Same as us. They called the coroner. He pronounced Morgan Mason dead, phoned a funeral parlor to pick him up, and authorized an autopsy. Ari will do it on Monday."

I knew Aristotle Papas from his trial testimony over the years. Ari *made* the news; I *covered* it. I liked him very much. So did Sebastian, who always cleverly managed to arrive at the morgue's dissection room just after an autopsy had been performed.

No fool he.

Although he and Ari weren't exactly drinking buddies, they had worked together on several cases and were on a first-name basis. Ari was a tall man, slightly myopic behind old-fashioned tortoise-shell eyeglasses, with a high forehead and a thin, affable face. Sebastian appreciated the forensic pathologist's good mind and willingness to go that extra step or perform that extra test. Sebastian also got a kick out of Ari's fussiness, manifested by his scrupulous neatness, his immaculate button-down shirts, his perky bow ties, and his brilliantly shined shoes.

Billy calls him "the Anti-Death."

I turned to my brother.

He was sitting a little too upright at the table with his eyes closed. I thought he was asleep, so I poked him.

His eyes flew open.

Once a fireman, always a fireman.

Billy gave me a brotherly kiss on the cheek, stood up, said, "Night, Annie," and ambled sleepily toward the guest room. I called out after him, "I've got to do some scut work for the newspaper, but I'll be back before dinner."

Then I gently removed the coffee cup from Sebastian's hand. My decrepit darling continued to talk, but it was sleep talking.

"We left a trooper at the Skirt Man's house."

I grabbed both of his hands, hauled him to his feet, and led him toward the stairs. When we got there, I gave him a booster push from behind, which was good practice in case I ever decide to become a Sherpa guide.

"What else?" I asked.

"Nothing much. It's my case. We retained possession of the scene."

"You and Billy will figure out what happened."

"Annie, I am really tired."

"Yes, sweetheart. I know."

"I've got to take a shower."

"Don't bother. We can always burn the sheets."

Sebastian stopped at the head of the stairs. He said, rallying to stay awake, "I was at a fire scene, Annie. There was a DOA. I *have* to take a shower."

I looked at him. My darling, scrupulous husband. I understood. Ugliness. Nastiness. Death. Down the drain.

"Okay," I agreed. "I'll monitor the proceedings and make sure you don't drown."

"Thank you, Annie." Sebastian's eyes closed for a moment. I woke him up and led him toward the bathroom.

"What about the dog?" I asked.

He shuffled forward. "One of the pathologists at Cornell specializes in animal autopsies."

"He's doing Buddy?"

"She. Sometime this week."

The door to the bathroom opened.

Merry stood in the doorway. Her big brown eyes were shining with life. Her ivory skin was glowing with health.

There was one bath towel wrapped around her slender body and another binding her bright red hair.

"Hi, Mom," she sang out. "Hi, Daddy. I'll be dressed in a minute."

She disappeared into her bedroom.

But before Sebastian or I had taken another step, she poked her head out again and said, "By the way, Daddy, there's a goat in your bed."

chapter 8

I GUESS NOW would be as good a time as any to tell you about Slim Cornfield, the editor in chief, publisher, and owner of the *County Courier and Gazette*. Slim was a forty-two-year-old, never-married, lifelong resident of Killdeer, and he was having—how can I put this delicately—a post-millennium meltdown.

He had called me into his office a week before the town hall benefit at the ungodly hour of eight o'clock in the morning. His briefcase was open on his desk and as he talked he was throwing into it an argyle sock (just one); a dark purple amethyst crystal geode; a small hourglass filled with white sand; a how-to book on identifying spiders; a bottle of calamine lotion, and a leather-bound journal.

Well, he had *started* to pack the journal. Then he pulled it out and clutched it fiercely in his hands.

"Annie, you gave me this the year you came to work here. How long ago was that?"

I thought back. Merry was nineteen years old now and I had come to the *Gazette* the year before she entered our lives.

I was about to answer Slim's question, but he cut me off. "Twenty years ago."

He held the journal in front of me—literally under my nose, opening it to the cover page, on which a few lines had been written in my handwriting. Slim pretended to be reading them, but his eyes never left mine, so I knew that he had memorized the words.

"Dear Boss," he recited. "May this diary be a record of the Lewis and Clark expedition of your life, its loves, journeys, accomplishments, and adventures. Happy Christmas from the new kid on the block. Annie Bly."

Then Slim slowly flipped through the pages.

The empty, empty pages.

"Since you gave this to me, Annie, *you* have been involved in catching a murderess, adopting a child, building a solid marriage to Sebastian, and solving crimes with your brother. *You* have gone back and forth to visit your parents in Wyoming and back and forth to your apartment in Manhattan. *You* have helped to launch the career of a daughter who, by all accounts, is destined to be a great dancer. *You* have a husband who worships you, a kid who adores you, and a boss you can wrap around your little finger. You also have had fun."

He tossed the journal into the briefcase.

"Deny it," he demanded.

Obviously, my repressed, self-effacing geek of a boss had lost his mind and had already written the dialogue for the scene we were playing.

Equally obvious, I had enough sense to read from his script.

"I can't deny it," I said, as noncombustibly as I could.

Slim slammed down the lid of the briefcase. Keep in mind that Slim was not a lid-slamming kind of guy.

"Since that Christmas, all *I* have done is run a newspaper I inherited from my father."

He walked to the window of his office and looked out at the uninspiring view of a lumberyard across the parking lot from the *County Courier and Gazette*.

Slim raised one arm above his head and rested it against the window frame. I had to move closer to hear what he said next, which I recognized as a stanza from a Robert Wilson Service poem. Slim's voice was low, but infused with a strength and intensity I had never heard in it before, as he said:

> *There's a race of men that don't fit in,*
> *A race that can't stay still;*
> *So they break the hearts of kith and kin*
> *And they roam the world at will.*

Slim turned. His eyes strayed in my direction, but I can't say that he was really looking at me.

"You see, Annie." His voice was still oddly and uncharacteristically strong. "When I got up this morning, I realized . . . or maybe the word is *faced* . . . that not only had I *not* roamed the world at will, I also had never found a heart I could break even if I wanted to. The only part of the poem that applies to me is the one about not fitting in."

Then Slim Cornfield's eyes came into focus and he looked right at me. That was when I noticed, notwithstanding his nerdy short-sleeved shirts and the pocket shield for his leaking ballpoint pens, that Slim was really a handsome man. Tall and slim, of course. Hence the nickname. His pants were always rumpled, his shoes were always scuffed, and his cracked leather belt was probably a relic from his days as an Eagle Scout. But he had nice, thick, sandy brown hair and appealing stuck-out ears. His face was what I can only describe as quintessentially American. The kind you would see on the barnstormers of the early twentieth century or the lads boarding troopships to fight Nazis during World War II. It was a boy's face, incapable of malice, matured nicely to accommodate a man who had never quite known how to inhabit it.

He said bitterly, his eyes not leaving mine:

> *There's a race of men that don't fit in,*
> *That never roams at will.*
> *They have no heart, no kith nor kin,*
> *A race that just sits still.*

He took his appointment calendar off his desk and held it up. "Meetings with reporters, photographers, printers, paper salesmen, ink distributors, computer repairmen, graphic designers, the mayor, the town supervisor, the chairman of the canoe regatta, advertisers, bankers, the Rotary Club, the Sertoma Society, and the Chamber of Commerce. No wife's birthday. No wife. No kids' birthdays. No kids. Parents dead. No friends. No time for friends."

He tossed the appointment calendar into the wastebasket, stood behind his desk, leaned forward on his knuckles, and stared at me.

"Here's the deal," he said. "I am selling the newspaper."

I gasped.

"To a syndicate."

I double gasped.

"Unless you sit down in my chair right now and assume the dubious honor of being the *Courier's* editor in chief."

I stood. Mute. Stunned.

Slim undid the strap of his wristwatch, easily as old as his belt, and tossed that in the wastebasket, too. It clinked against the spine of the appointment calendar.

He walked around his desk and stood next to me. I looked up.

"I never realized before how tall you are," I said, stupidly.

He put one hand on each of my shoulders and led me—pushed me, actually—behind his desk. Then he pressed down on my shoulders and, next thing you know, I was sitting in the seat of the editor in chief.

Me. Little Miss Don't Bother Me with Responsibility.

Me. The Mistress of Thanks, But No Thanks.

Me. The Short-Brain Queen.

He left me there and assumed the spot where I had been standing.

"How long will you be gone?" I asked.

"Maybe forever."

"What are you going to do?"

Slim shrugged. "Take a freighter to Hong Kong. Save a damsel in distress. Clean out my attic. Learn how to fly a helicopter. Take fencing lessons. Sell the house. Become a farmer. Move to Manhattan. I don't know, Annie. All I know is that if I stay here one more minute, I'll die a dried-up, lonely old man, and I am not going to do that to myself."

"How do I . . ." I started.

Slim reached into his pocket, took out a bundle of keys, and threw them on his desk.

"You're a big girl," he said. "Figure it out."

Then, looking, I have to admit, positively renewed, he strode out of his . . . my . . . our office.

chapter 9

WHICH IS WHY I had to do the scut work I mentioned to Billy and Sebastian when I put them to bed. Specifically, the work involved writing a series of articles on the history of the Killdeer Town Hall auditorium.

Had my downhearted and truculent boss not gone into soul-makeover mode, I could have stayed at home contemplating the inherent virtues of snoring men. Instead, I was on my way to pick up old articles and photographs from Lillian Roadigger, who, as I mentioned before, was not only a public health nurse but also the Killdeer town historian.

I had known Lillian by sight for almost ten years, but we hadn't become friendly until my manicurist moved from Fawn Creek to Killdeer and Lillian started to have her nails done at the same time and place as I. In fact, Lillian Roadigger, Rose Gimbel (the town tax assessor, about whom I will tell you more later), and I occasionally scheduled our manicures concurrently to catch up on gossip.

Although Lillian didn't have any outstanding features, or even a particularly well-put-together face, there was a piquant something about her, and the overall effect was of a woman who is pretty, feminine, and petite. She had nicely arched eyebrows that gave her a look of semi-astonishment, a short cap of curly blond hair, and tiny, perfect ears. Until fairly recently, Lillian had always looked sad to me. No, that's not quite right. Just markedly not happy, as opposed to *un*happy.

Sebastian's analysis is that she was a late bloomer who had suddenly burst into flower, which is as good an explanation as any. I leaned toward the theory that she was so relieved her children had finally left home that the happiness positively radiated out of her.

Regardless of what precipitated the change, it had been great fun for me to watch Lillian captivate the audience at the town hall the night before, and if I wasn't overjoyed by the prospect of picking up the archival material I needed for the article that I didn't want to write, I wasn't exactly dreading it either.

I had never been to the Roadigger house before I pulled into her driveway. Nor had I met Lillian's husband, Vernon. I knew that he had retired a few years back as vice president of sales for a company that made tongue depressors, and I thought it must have been hysterically funny to have to admit *that* at a cocktail party.

Lillian came to the door before I even rang the bell.

"Annie," she said hurriedly, her face looking pale and drawn. "I tried to call and cancel, but your daughter said you had already left. Do come in, though. I'm afraid I only have a minute, because I have the most excruciating headache, and it just won't go away."

I immediately started to tell Lillian that we could put off my visit for another day, but she grabbed my arm and dragged me into the hall.

"I've already prepared a folder for you, Annie. If you're

looking for anything I didn't put inside, give me a call later in the week." Then she turned and began to walk quickly toward the back of the house.

I followed her through a rather uncongenial living room, with dark brown sofas, angular chairs, and boxy mahogany furniture. We continued down a short hall through a spotless kitchen, and finally stopped at a nice-sized sunroom that positively glittered with life. There were diamond and heart-shaped crystal prisms hanging in wide windows between lush asparagus ferns and spider plants, and on each windowsill were rows of jolly looking potted violets, each containing bright purple, lavender, or pink blooms.

A large, round oak table dominating the center of the room was cluttered with an amalgam of yellowing newspaper clippings, family photo albums, sepia photographs, vintage calendars, and file folders. Lillian lifted three of these from a pile and handed them to me.

"It would be nice if you mentioned that the town hall will be celebrating its centennial in four years," Lillian said. "It had been neglected for decades until 1976 when the Killdeer Arts Council was formed. Initially the council was created to save the theater. But later—"

Lillian cut herself off with a pained "Oooh!"

Her hand flew up and she pressed her fingers against her forehead for a few long moments. When she dropped her hand, her skin was chalky white and the expression on her face was as ghastly as the aftermath of a scream.

"You look terrible," I said. "Walk me to the door and then go to bed."

Lillian nodded.

As we retraced our steps, things began to register in my mind that I had missed on my way in. I particularly noted that, with the exception of the sunroom, the house had all the animation of a blueprint. The kitchen was a nightmare of gleaming aluminum and spotless white tile with nothing on the counter but five maniacally polished pipes in a black enamel rack. There were no magazines or newspapers tossed about. There were no afghans casually draped over the arms of chairs. No throw pillows and no knickknacks. Books were lined up on bookshelves by the color of their bindings and the height of their spines. Windows were covered not by curtains or drapes but by antiseptic venetian blinds. The only ornamentations on the walls were two framed photographs of Lillian's children. I didn't know their names, but I remembered them as humorless teenagers who had worked behind the counter after school at the pharmacy. The boy, dark eyed and dour. The girl, also dour, with light blue eyes that had black rims around the irises. Memorable eyes that should have been beautiful but were not.

Just as I was about to open the front door to go outside, I barely avoided colliding with a man coming in. He was in his late sixties and resembled the less-than-elated looking children whose photographs were on the wall.

"Vernon," Lillian's voice was low and a little shaky. "This is Annie Bly. She made the trip here to get some material on the town hall. I had wanted to show her your gardens before she left, but I have a dreadful headache. Would you mind . . ."

The sentence drifted off as Lillian waited for her husband's response.

Vernon was short. As short as she was. He had pewter-colored hair, furry black eyebrows, tufts of hair in his ears, and small black eyes. The skin on his face was loose, but his mouth was tight, as if his kindergarten teacher had said sixty years ago, "Zip up your lip," and he hadn't unzipped it since.

He looked at me briefly. For all the interest he showed, I could have been a Tupperware bowl. My eyes dropped to a white handkerchief wrapped around the handle of the thing he was leaning on.

Seeing the flick of my eyes, he barked, "Arthritis."

Then he added, "Come with me."

I turned to say good-bye to Lillian, but she had already disappeared. So I shrugged and followed the lord of the manor into the yard.

The farmer's overalls Vernon was wearing should have been the tip-off. As soon as I saw them, I ought to have suspected that his gardens would be Serious Endeavors.

They were.

All three of them. Two behind the house. One behind the garage. Each was approximately sixty feet deep by forty feet wide, and each was filled with meticulous row after row of practical things like radishes, rhubarb, cucumbers, and string beans. The two gardens behind the house grew vegetables; the one behind the garage grew herbs. At the head of each row in each garden were thin spikes driven into the ground and topped with small plaques on which someone had written: LETTUCE. ZUCCHINI. TOMATO. BROCCOLI. KALE.

The rows were militaristically parallel and made me pine for a little imperfection—a nice, sloppy pumpkin vine breaking rank and ravishing the radishes. But that was not to be in this geometric compilation of agricultural artifacts where I was certain no deer dared to graze, no rabbit risked a nibble, and slugs tucked in their tails and slithered off to gardens more amenable to their slime.

I continued to follow Vernon as he hobbled briskly from row to row and garden to garden. Now and again I murmured appreciative insincerities about how nice it all was, which seemed to please that grim little man to no end.

When I had finally retreated to the driveway and opened the door of my car to make my escape, Vernon said, "One second, please, Mrs. Bly," and he hurried off behind the barn. Less than three minutes later, he returned, carrying a basket of assorted green things. He pressed this cornucopia into my arms, all the while assuring me that the spiky object with the outrageously hairy leaves needed only a dash of vinegar to bring out the flavor and that an oblong, rooty-looking thing had to be boiled in water for an hour and fifteen minutes before it was peeled.

My disingenuous responses must have been provoked by a skill I didn't know I possessed because, by the time I was pulling out of the driveway, Vernon Roadigger's mouth had unzipped enough for me to see, if not a smile, at least the absence of a frown.

chapter 10

MY BROTHER WOKE UP that Sunday afternoon while I was still out tracking down research material for my story. Billy always takes dozens of pictures at a fire scene and had driven to a one-hour photo lab in Norwich. Part of his training of new fire investigators is to tell them, over and over again, that film is cheap.

And so, on the night of the fire at the Skirt Man's house, he took four rolls of film and thirty-two more pictures with his back-up digital camera. Sebastian was also away from the house when I got back. He had gone to Troop C headquarters to write his report, and he was still there when I turned into the driveway. Billy pulled in a minute or two later. Just as I threw my purse on a chair, the screen door crashed open and Billy charged through. Before he had even said hello, he spread out his pictures on the kitchen table and said, "Come here, Annie. Take a look."

Now let me make this perfectly clear. I am not a fan of crime-scene paraphernalia and I have an immutable aversion to anything that can no longer respire, perspire, or buy me jewelry. However, in my capacity as the *County Courier and Gazette*'s reluctant editor in chief, I felt that it was my duty to view the postmortem fire scene photographs.

They were pretty bad.

Billy went over them with me one by one, and he told me much more than I ever wanted to know about what happened to someone unfortunate enough to be burned in a fire.

"Heat causes the body to dehydrate and the muscles to shrink," he explained. "As a result, the arms and legs of a fire victim are often found in a pugilistic, boxer-like pose."

That had not happened to the Skirt Man, though.

I could see in the photos that what was left of him was sprawled over what was left of the chair that he had been sitting on.

It was really quite freaky.

Being the sister of a fire marshal and the nosy wife of a state police investigator, I had seen photographs of dead people before. But I had never seen anything as bad as this. There was no skin. No nose. No ears. No lips. No cheeks. No fingers. No toes. Nothing but blackened tendons covered a pathetic compilation of bones—a limp, prone, horrible *thing* that had once been a shy but likable farmer who had a dog, drove a tractor, and stuttered.

Billy pointed to a zigzag on a close-up of the Skirt Man's skull and said it was a heat fracture. He added that he was going to ask Dr. Pappas to x-ray the entire body to look for bullets and have him pay particular attention to any damage that might have occurred in the area where the base of the skull meets the spine—a place that looked ruptured to him, but where heat fractures do not normally occur.

Assuming there was enough tissue left, Billy said, Dr. Pappas would also test for the presence of carbon monoxide in the blood. If there was any carbon monoxide present, it meant that Morgan Mason was alive before the fire started. If there was none, he already would have been dead.

As I somberly sorted through the rest of his photographs, Billy explained that there were six ways in which a person could be burned.

"The first," he said, "is flame impingement. That happens when a body comes into contact with actual flames. The second is a contact burn. If you touch a hot surface like the bottom of an iron or a skillet on a stove, you get a contact burn. The third type is a radiant heat burn. That kind of burn is caused by electromagnetic heat waves. If I'm stuck in a room that's on fire, even if I don't come into contact with flames, I can get a radiant heat burn. Overexposure to a sunlamp is another kind of radiant heat burn. We'll skip over the last three types of burns because they didn't come into play here, but for the record, they're scalding, chemical burns, and microwave burns."

Billy reached into the pile of pictures and pulled out a particularly horrific one, where blacked tissue had split open, exposing a raw, red gash over grayish white bone. The chest and abdominal walls also seemed to have been burned away, and I saw more of Morgan Mason's internal organs than I wanted to.

It was really depressing.

"All of these burns," Billy said, "were from flame impingement."

He let the photograph drop back on the pile and looked at me.

"Annie, what do you know about cremation?"

"Nothing. Which is all I want to know."

"The temperature inside a house fire," he went on, ignoring me, "usually tops off at around 1,600 degrees Fahrenheit.

You need a temperature of about 2,000 degrees Fahrenheit to cremate a body."

"Two thousand degrees for how long?" I pretended to be interested.

"Complete cremation might take up to two-and-a-half hours."

I glanced at the photograph that Billy had just dropped.

"No," he answered the question I hadn't asked. "Morgan Mason was not cremated, but the chair he was sitting on came pretty damn close to being a funeral pyre."

He flipped through the pictures and pulled out four of the living room that showed the charred stubs and coiled-spring remnants of the chair, as well as parts of the two adjoining walls. They were taken after the Skirt Man's body had been removed. Billy partially overlapped the left side of one photograph with the right side of another until he had created a panorama of three sides of the room.

"You've seen fire photos before, Annie. What strikes you as being odd or different about this?"

I studied the fire scene.

Layman that I am, even I couldn't help but notice that other than the debris left behind by the chair, the room itself was almost untouched by fire.

I turned to Billy.

"Pretty localized, right?"

"I'd say so."

"What do you think happened?"

"I think that the Skirt Man was murdered."

"How?"

"I don't know the answer to that yet, Annie."

"Then why was he killed?"

"When I figure out how, I'll know why."

I thought about that for a minute.

"Okay, someone shot him," I said. "Or poisoned, or stabbed, or whacked him on the head. Then what?"

Billy indicated the remnant of a chair leg. "Then they dragged or carried him to the chair, dumped him into it, and set it on fire."

"With flammable liquid?"

"Didn't need an accelerant. Not with a chair like this, stuffed with dried-out cotton batting and covered with material so old it's ready to disintegrate. I've said it before, Annie. It was a funeral pyre. The bad guy could have ignited the fabric around the base or put a few crumpled-up sheets of newspaper on the floor under the frame and let it burn up from there. If we factor in the cloth from the skirt that Morgan Mason was wearing, there would have been one hell of a fuel load."

I pulled over the photographs so that they were on the table directly in front of me and again I started to thumb through them, going past one, doing a mental double take, and bringing it back.

My voice was cautious, as if I were afraid that if I drew attention to what I was looking at, the object might disappear.

"Billy, is that . . . ?"

My brother leaned over. His analytical skills were so fine tuned that he instantly dropped his finger where I had been staring.

"Good catch, Annie," he said. "It's a pipe."

"A tobacco pipe?"

"Right again. We found it under Morgan Mason's body when he was being transferred to the body bag."

I looked up.

"Then maybe . . ."

"Maybe what, Annie?"

"Maybe the Skirt Man wasn't murdered. Maybe he fell

asleep when he was smoking his pipe. Maybe his pipe dropped between the cushions, and what you called the funeral pyre he was sitting on just burst into flames."

My brother lifted the picture off the pile. The pipe in the photograph was so badly burned that it looked like one of those licorice pipes candy stores used to sell to children.

Billy shook his head. His sky-blue eyes glinted cynically.

"That's exactly what the bad guy wants us to think."

chapter 11

I WOULD LOVE TO impress everyone with tales of how I turned Vernon Roadigger's leafy largesse into a culinary masterpiece, but, in fact, I contributed it, roots and all, to Merry's goat. He, by the way, (the pink ribbon had been misleading), had not really been in our bed. Exhibiting an uncharacteristic flippancy that I am sure was influenced by the Dillenbeck duo, Merry had made a joke.

This pygmy creature—Merry named him Livingston—had taken up residence in the barn. At least, he was there whenever he wasn't in our kitchen being petted on Merry's diminutive lap.

When Sebastian got home that Sunday night, he did a quick job of going through Billy's photographs. After dinner, no one was in the mood for serious conversation so Billy turned on the television set to *Heaven and Earth,* thinking that, at worst, it would be harmlessly amusing.

Up until that moment, Morgan Mason's death had been distressing to his friends, disturbing to his neighbors, and sad for the rest of us.

Heaven and Earth transformed it into a nightmare.

"Jesus Christ!" Billy exclaimed as he stared at the television. "Is there any way we can tape this?"

Merry, who was the only one of us who knew how to work the recording thingy on the TV, leaped forward and pressed a series of buttons.

"Done, Uncle Billy."

"We're recording?"

"Yes."

Then she sat down next to my brother on the sofa while Sebastian and I hurried to position ourselves. Sebastian sat next to Merry. I sat on the floor with my arms wrapped around my husband's legs. We stared in horror at the scene unfolding before us.

From the music, the video montage, and Creedmore Snowdon's sepulchral voiceover, I knew that the show was just beginning.

I had seen *Heaven and Earth* many times before because it was fun to watch disembodied heads, green mists, and genetic mutations drift across the screen; it also was entertaining to see someone we knew and disliked make an inoffensive fool of himself.

That night Snowdon Creedmore was neither inoffensive nor foolish.

He and his show became dangerous.

"*Spontaneous human combustion,*" he intoned as an obviously hand-held camera slowly panned a fire-damaged room.

"*Disparaged by scoffers as unscientific—*"

"That's the Skirt Man's house." Billy expelled a low snarl.

"*—lauded by believers as irrefutable—*"

The camera cut to a dark heap of debris on what appeared to be a living-room floor. A series of quick cuts followed, each of such short duration that the viewer could not confirm and did not want to believe what he was seeing.

Could that possibly be the charred remains of a leg?

Is that a femur sticking out from what had once been a thigh?

Can that disfigured claw really be all that is left of a human hand?

But it went by too fast.

For half a second, we were sure we were looking at bits and pieces of a partially incinerated human being. A brief second later, we were doubting our own perceptions and senses.

We stared at the television set, eyes unblinking, minds numb.

Sebastian leaned forward.

"That bastard videotaped Morgan Mason before he—"

"*And now,*" Creedmore's funereal voice continued. "*With footage taken only yesterday of this previously unverified phenomenon, spontaneous human combustion has been proven beyond any possibility of doubt.*"

More seared body parts flashed on and off the screen in a sequence suggestive of a macabre striptease. But no charred tissue, heat fracture, or exposed bone remained visible long enough for certainty to set in, and at the exact moment you were about to protest against the ghoulish display, the exploded skull that you *thought* you were looking at seemed to evolve into a clot of burned carpet or a charred bit of cloth.

As those barely recognizable images continued to disappear and reappear, Creedmore Snowdon introduced a series of photographs illustrating earlier cases of spontaneous human combustion and he tied them to various theories, which he said explained the phenomenon.

I can't remember—and wouldn't want to—the basis of any of these hypotheses, but I do dimly recollect phrases such as "quantum theory of neutrinos" and "crematorium effect" and "malignant hypothermia" and "death by internal ignition."

Or, as Billy so disdainfully summarized it, "Gobbledy-gook."

My favorite of the case histories presented was what I call the Mysterious Incineration of Madge.

The circumstances were these:

Lucy, aged eighteen, had come to live with her Aunt Madge after her parents died in a car crash. An ambitious girl, Lucy had big dreams, all of which involved moving as far away from her aunt as the continent allowed. Madge, however, was more than content to keep pretty Lucy within beck-ing and calling distance, since doing so was an economical and expeditious way for her to have her house cleaned, her meals cooked, her cigarettes lighted, and her gin purchased, poured, and delivered to the ground-floor bedroom where she read romance novels sixteen hours a day.

Did I forget to mention that the lady of the house had at-tained the proportions, if not the grace, of a sumo wrestler?

Anyway...

It transpired—according to Creedmore Snowdon and il-lustrated by various photographs of rooms and debris not dissimilar to those taken at the Skirt Man's house—that one chilly Sunday evening at exactly 7:44 P.M., after having poured her aunt a nice slug of gin and retiring to the kitchen, Lucy smelled smoke. She ran down the hall to Madge's bedroom, pushed open the door, and was stunned to discover that only twenty-nine minutes after Lucy had last seen her, both Aunt Madge and the chair she was sitting on had been almost com-pletely consumed by a violent and self-extinguishing fire.

I say "almost," because something did remain of Madge. At the base of what had once been her chair were a pair of singed feet, stuffed into the charred residue of two leather slippers.

What had happened to the rest of Madge?

Spontaneous human combustion, of course!

"Not half an hour ago, dear Aunt Madge was as perky as a tulip poking its head out of the ground in the spring." Lucy wept, her eyelashes fluttering furiously with tears.

"Yep," retired Fire Marshal Kevin Darling confirmed in a videotaped interview, nodding his head in baffled agreement. "Darnedest thing I ever saw. One minute she's there. Next she's gone. Nothing left of Madge but her feet. Chair's gone, too. Burned to cinders like a marshmallow over a campfire. In under thirty minutes. Even with her being a smoker and drinking gin like she did." He stopped nodding his head and began to shake it. "There are things here that I just can't account for."

"Tulips. Marshmallows." Billy yelled at the television. "Lucy is a killer, you gullible moron!"

Billy's explanation of Madge's near-total extinction was simplicity itself.

One: Lucy had lied about everything.

Two: Lucy had murdered Madge, dismembered her body, and buried it, except for the feet, at some undisclosed location.

Three: Lucy had placed Madge's slipper-clad, disembodied feet on the thickly upholstered chair in the bedroom and set fire to the chair.

Four: Boo-hooing every carefully planned step along the way, Lucy then called the fire department and reported Aunt Madge's miraculous and almost complete incineration.

"Son of a bitch," Sebastian exclaimed, reaching for the telephone.

"What, Daddy?" Merry asked, eager, as we all were, to find out what Sebastian intended to do.

"That guy."

"Who?"

"The television guy. Creedmore Snowdon."

"What about him?"

Sebastian punched in the numbers for the Chenango County District Attorney.

"I'm getting a court order for him to produce every inch of footage he videotaped when he contaminated, *contaminated* my crime scene. And . . ."

"And what?"

"He's just jumped to the top of my list of suspects."

chapter 12

HYPOTHETICAL SITUATION:

There is a fire at Myra and Phil Huckleberry's house and someone calls in an alarm.

Hypothetical response to hypothetical situation:

The fire engine arrives and the fire department takes possession of the scene.

This means that if Mrs. Huckleberry says to the chief in charge that she simply *must* go inside to retrieve her great grandmother's cameo broach, the water-sogged album containing her wedding photos, or her insurance policy, she will not be permitted to step across her own threshold if the fire chief says, "No."

Mrs. Huckleberry may own the house, but she does not own the fire scene.

The fire department does.

Let's say that shortly after the fire has been put out, one of the firemen pulls the chief aside and says, "We smelled gasoline in the back bedroom, and when we put water on the flames, they flared back up."

The chief follows the fireman into the back bedroom, pokes around a bit, and puts in a call to the fire marshal, the sheriff's department, the city police, or whomever is responsible in that jurisdiction for determining the origin and cause of a fire.

When the fire investigators arrive, the chief relates his suspicions that they could be dealing with a deliberately set fire. He answers any questions the investigators might have. Then he orders his men to take up their equipment and leave, in effect transferring possession of the fire scene to the fire marshals.

If Myra Huckleberry now proclaims that her only goal in life is to go into her house and remove one small envelope from a readily accessible kitchen drawer, she cannot do so while the fire marshals have the scene. Nor can her husband go inside for his golf shoes, nor can her insurance adjuster enter the premises to begin his inventory, nor can the fire expert employed by her insurance company go inside to start his origin-and-cause investigation.

No one may enter the Huckleberry residence until the fire marshals are through with it. Those particular specialists *own* the scene, and during the time when they do, they are mandated by the city, county, or state that employs them to make every effort to answer two questions.

Where did the fire start?

What precipitated the fire?

Its origin and its cause.

My brother Billy had gone to great pains to explain to me that, even though origin and cause may sometimes seem to be inextricably intertwined, they are actually two very separate and distinct determinations.

A fire on a kitchen countertop might have started in the same corner where Myra Huckleberry kept the toaster, but that does not necessarily mean the toaster was the cause of the fire.

Maybe there was a short circuit in the wall outlet that the toaster was plugged into.

Maybe the house was struck by lightning or hit by a power surge that fried the wires inside the walls and caused flames to break through the sheetrock behind the toaster.

Maybe Myra Huckleberry was a chain smoker and she carelessly left a cigarette smoldering on the countertop when she was preparing toast.

Or maybe the elevator arm of the toaster got stuck in the DOWN position, the thermal cutoff failed, and the toaster really did cause the fire.

Every plausible scenario has to be considered.

A fire marshal, however, is primarily concerned with crime. If and when he makes the determination that ignition and combustion were the result of an accident, his interest subsides, and he would say to Mr. and Mrs. Huckleberry, "I'm done here. It's all yours."

But if a fireman really *had* smelled gasoline and if the burn patterns in the back bedroom confirmed that someone had indeed poured a flammable liquid between the nightstand and the bed, then the fire investigation becomes an arson investigation and the fire scene becomes a crime scene.

In New York City, fire marshals are law-enforcement officers and can retain control of a premise until their investigations are complete. Fire investigators with no police powers, however, have to turn their cases over to the police. Either way, Mrs. Huckleberry, her husband, her insurance agent, and her adjuster would not be permitted to put a foot inside the property until the fire scene, which is now a crime scene, has been relinquished.

In the case of the Skirt Man's fire, Sebastian had posted a

trooper outside the house to protect the premises and maintain a log of anyone who tried to enter or leave. A state trooper would remain there until the investigation was completed.

These procedures became particularly relevant in the hours following the broadcast of *Heaven and Earth*.

At no time during the course of the show had Creedmore Snowdon specifically identified Morgan Mason as the fire victim. Nor had he given the address where the fire had occurred. But everyone who was watching the show in Killdeer recognized the Skirt Man's house, and they told friends and family, who told more friends and family, who told other acquaintances in other towns and cities, and before long, local TV stations and not-so-local newspapers were sending reporters to interrogate the people in our area.

Or, at least, they tried to.

They failed.

Why?

Because independently and unanimously, with no forethought and without the organizational momentum of a town resolution, each and every person in Killdeer who was approached by a TV reporter, cameraman, or journalist decided to lie.

A terrible misfortune had befallen one of their own, and they were not about to let anyone exploit it.

"What do you know about the guy who died in the fire?" one reporter inquired of Alf Lubbock, who made pizzas over at Mario's Ristorante.

"I never heard of him," Alf quickly responded.

A different reporter approached Bonnie Woodruff, a checkout clerk at the Bargain Rite Grocery.

"His name was Mason. Morgan Mason. Supposedly he died of spontaneous human combustion."

"Morgan Mason?" Bonnie repeated meditatively. "Sounds

like a character in a movie. Are you sure someone's not pulling your leg?"

Other townspeople who were approached were equally unresponsive.

"Where did the old guy live?"

"What old guy?"

"The one who died in the fire."

"What fire?"

"The one of Saturday night."

"There wasn't a fire on Saturday night."

"Some people say that he wore a skirt."

"Ha. In a small town like this, you think we wouldn't notice an old guy wearing a skirt?"

"I hear he lived over on Route 39."

"Well, you heard wrong."

A few of the reporters who weren't stonewalled were creatively misdirected.

"Oh, yeah. I heard of a guy like that in Delaware County. Why don't you try looking over by the Cannonsville Reservoir?"

"We had a fellow who burned to death just like you said. But that was during the Mormon migration over a hundred years ago."

"Yep. There's a guy who lives down in Franklin. He wears a real pretty skirt and two earrings in his left ear, and he's got a big old belly and a beard clear down to his belt buckle. Last I heard, he was making jewelry out of old tin cans. Why don't you give him a call? He can tell you if he's dead or not."

After a day of this, most of the newshounds packed up and went home. Some, however—the ones who had gotten their information directly from Creedmore Snowdon or Decidia Skirball—were given the address of the Skirt Man's house.

The state trooper who had been assigned to protect the premises was able to keep the reporters from getting inside.

But he wasn't able to stop gawkers and photographers from parking their cars on the shoulder of the road, trampling the Skirt Man's gardens, taking pictures of his house, and telling tales.

Pictures of what, though?

What had really happened?

An old and unimportant farmer was dead. Nobody had proved that he was the victim of a crime, and despite the furor created by *Heaven and Earth,* producers of serious news shows were not about to broadcast pseudo-scientific speculations about how the Skirt Man had died in the fire.

In effect, nothing of an earth-shattering nature had happened and there wasn't much of a story to tell.

Two days after the hubbub that had been precipitated by *Heaven and Earth* began, all of the journalists left town. By the third morning, interest in the fire and the Skirt Man had fallen off sharply and the people of Killdeer were able to go back to being the honest or dishonest folk they had always been.

chapter 13

BECAUSE THE Hobby Hills Horse Farm bore the same relationship to Killdeer that a malignant tumor does to a lung, Sebastian and Billy began their investigation by going there and interviewing Domingo Nogales Ramirez on the Monday morning after the fire.

It is difficult for many of the old-timers in the area to view Hobby Hills with the revulsion it deserves because for a very long time it occupied such a pleasant place in our memories. Even for Sebastian and me. We didn't buy Merry's horse, Clementine, at Hobby Hills, but we had gone there for just about every other horse-related necessity, including saddles, feed, and riding lessons.

"Don't waste your money," Ruth Sterner said after our daughter's second lesson. "Merry must have been born on a horse."

Ruth Sterner and her husband, Ned, had owned the Hobby Hills Horse Farm since Noah kicked them off the ark with the command to bear fruit and multiply. The horses had obeyed. Ruth and Ned had not. They died childless about twelve years ago. Shortly afterward, the executors of their estate put the farm up for sale.

Unfortunately for the community, Domingo Nogales Ramirez bought it.

Maybe...just maybe...Ramirez was not perfectly evil when he first started out. But he was a quick study. His original intention had been to run Hobby Hills as a campground. It had a farmhouse, two stables, and a barn on 212 acres of land, with a nice-sized lake surrounded by lush dogwood and evergreen trees.

Ramirez turned the stables into what he called "dormitory cabins"; stocked the lake with carp, catfish, and bass; built a small jetty; and bought ten dilapidated rowboats. He bribed a highway official so he could put up a sign on Interstate 57 identifying Hobby Hills as a campsite, and then he ran classified ads offering summer rentals of "beautiful lakeside cabins for the entire family."

For almost a decade, Domingo Nogales Ramirez made money. Then word got out that Hobby Hills was little more than a summer slum and that people died there (seven drownings in less than five years). As corpse upon corpse piled up, the people in Killdeer started to call the fatal body of water in Hobby Hills "Death Lake," and began to wonder why their city officials were behaving as though they had become terminally hard of hearing, if not completely deaf to the outrages that were being perpetrated there.

When seven able-bodied adults die within a short period of time in any given location, those deaths should raise eyebrows at the very least. That all of the deaths were attributed to boating accidents while under the influence of alcohol should not only have raised eyebrows, it should have rung bells, shattered glass, and precipitated a multi-jurisdictional investigation.

For some reason, however, the fates of the fishermen who had camped, imbibed, and drowned at Hobby Hills were disassociated from the man who had created the place where it was so easy to die.

No summonses were issued.

No arrests were made.

No penalties or fines were imposed.

But people finally stopped coming to Hobby Hills, which meant that they stopped dying there, which meant that Domingo Ramirez was deprived of a source of income.

Not for long, though. He did a little research, called a few booking agents, and took out ads in counterculture magazines announcing that at the Hobby Hills Horse Farm (it amused him to still use the innocent-sounding name) Woodstock-like concerts would be held every weekend from Memorial Day to Labor Day. He hired bands with nasty names like Spitting Vengeance, Murder and Mayhem, and Severed Fingers, and a week after its reincarnation as a Rock Resort, Hobby Hills was making money again.

But this time, it was big money. Scary money. Drug money.

Each Friday afternoon, the Quick-It Mart on Route 7 became a way station for every emaciated, drugged out, boozed up, leftover hippy, beatnik, and teenaged wannabe punk rocker within a radius of five hundred miles. How they got to the Quick-It Mart is anyone's guess, but it was there that they stocked up on six-packs and from there that they drove, walked, or hitchhiked five more miles to the gated driveway of Hobby Hills.

A Night of Rock cost fifty dollars, payable in cash at the gate. It included free music and all the booze you could drink.

Depending on the band, the admission could go as high as ten times that.

Food, meaning potato chips, candy bars, and pizza, was extra. Mattresses were extra. Toilets were free, but always had a fifteen-minute line in front of them and were usually backed up, which is why Morgan Mason and others who lived nearby often found disgusting souvenirs in their yards where the drunken revelers had relieved themselves . . . or the drunken revelers themselves.

The sheriff's department estimated that each concert drew about a thousand people to Hobby Hills.

Dirty, rowdy, dangerous-looking people.

The music being blasted over the countryside from the former campsite's speakers was so loud that the state police and the sheriff's office received dozens of complaints every weekend.

Other locals, justifiably angry and dismayed, expressed concerns about the sanitation facilities at Hobby Hills, which had remained unchanged since it was a horse farm and were criminally inadequate to accommodate thousands of people.

Where was the sewage going?

Was it migrating into the local wells and contaminating the drinking water?

A brief flurry of official activity followed the initial spate of complaints. First, the Village of Killdeer issued fines to the Hobby Hills Horse Farm for health code violations; but they were so small that Domingo Ramirez arrogantly strode into the village office, laughed in the face of the village clerk, and paid the fines by throwing rolls of dimes, nickels, and quarters on her desk.

After that, the mayor of Killdeer asked the state police to set up checkpoints and roadblocks on Route 39 in order to search for drugs coming into or going out of the area.

In response, Domingo Ramirez hired a high-priced Manhattan lawyer who advised the village that his client would no longer tolerate being discriminated against because he was Puerto Rican (the name on his birth certificate was Franklin Matthew Ramirez, his mother was Dutch, he was born in Brooklyn, and he could only speak about six words of Spanish), and that if the harassment and the roadblocks continued, the Village of Killdeer could look forward to a million-dollar lawsuit.

The state police, I might add, were more than willing to continue the checkpoints and roadblocks. The mayor of Killdeer was not.

This was the state of affairs prior to the incident described by Sonny and Moses Dillenbeck in which the Skirt Man drove his tractor up the Hobby Hills driveway and had words with Domingo Ramirez.

One long-range consequence of this whole brouhaha, by the way, was that the people of Killdeer became so frustrated by their elected officials' inability or unwillingness to deal with the situation that the constituents of both political parties got into a snit and refused to nominate anyone to run for mayor.

The incumbent, a nice man whose day job had been renting videotapes at Marvelous Movies over by the railroad tracks, was so discouraged by the problems of his hometown that he quit his job, sold his snow blower, packed up his wife, and moved to Florida, which is why it had been so easy for Creedmore Snowdon, a newcomer, and Morgan Mason, an inarticulate, skirt-wearing farmer, to dominate their respective parties' campaigns.

All of this is a rather long beside the point, the point being that another possible consequence of the confrontation between Morgan Mason and Domingo Ramirez was that one of them was dead and the other was still thriving.

For all of those who, like me, fail to comprehend why the sheriff's department, the Killdeer Police Department (one part-time cop), or the state police had not intervened at Hobby Hills, the answer to that question is, "I still don't understand."

I'm not sure Sebastian does, either.

I do know that if more than 5,000 people attend an event and if the district attorney or the sheriff decide it is a threat to public health or safety, they can shut it down. Since Hobby Hills never drew more than a thousand people on any given occasion that option was out.

Being a public place, all an undercover cop had to do, in theory, was buy a ticket, walk into Hobby Hills, and as soon as he saw anyone dealing drugs, arrest him, her, or all of them.

So why wasn't that done?

When Sebastian was still a state trooper—before he was promoted to the Bureau of Criminal Investigation—he asked his lieutenant that very question half a dozen times.

He never got a straight answer.

Hobby Hills, he figured, just wasn't anybody's priority.

Not, at least, until the Monday morning after the Skirt Man's death, when he and Billy went to interview Domingo Ramirez.

Before they left, I pleaded with Sebastian to let me come along, assuring him that I would wear a Band-Aid across my mouth and swallow an invisibility pill. His unhusbandly response was an official state police "No."

All *that* accomplished was to postpone the inevitable, because when they came home on Monday night, I made them replay the whole interaction for me, gesture by gesture and line by line, starting with when they had pulled past the front gate.

———

IT WAS TEN O'CLOCK on Monday morning, July 18.

Sebastian and Billy drove up the circuitous driveway to the main buildings at Hobby Hills, passing bleary-eyed teenagers in clots of twos and threes who were stumbling down that same driveway toward Route 39. They pulled into the parking area in front of the main house. Just as they were getting out of their car, Domingo Nogales Ramirez jerked open the door to his house and stepped onto the porch.

"You're cops," he said gruffly. "What do you want?"

"Uh huh. Well, it's nice to meet you, too," Billy muttered under his breath.

Ramirez glared at him.

He had flat black eyes with opaque irises that completely filled the spaces between the lids. His eyebrows looked like strips of electrical tape. His upper eyelids were straight lines, and his lower lids were shallow semicircles that resembled drooping tea bags.

Wolves usually have a pretty extensive array of sheep's clothing.

Not Domingo Nogales Ramirez.

He looked like what he was. He had pockmarked skin, a big nose, puffy lips, and large ears that laid flat against his skull like suspects waiting to be patted down for hidden weapons.

He transferred his dark and depthless stare to Sebastian.

"Music too loud? Kids shitting on some old geezer's lawn? Jerks on motorcycles scaring old ladies who are trying to cross the street?" He snorted. A real snort. Like a bull or a pig. "If some idiot robs a gas station fifty miles away, you cops come here and try to lay the rap on me."

Sebastian looked down at his pants and brushed a speck of lint off his knee.

Billy tapped his foot and looked up at the sky.

They waited.

Ramirez, uncomfortable with the silence, barked, "Yeah? So?"

Sebastian let his eyes glide slowly toward the owner of Hobby Hills.

"This isn't about you, Mr. Ramirez," he said evenly.

"It's always about me."

"A neighbor of yours was found dead on Saturday night."

"Yeah? Well, my condolences. What's it got to do with me?"

"We understand that Morgan Mason came here recently to discuss events related to activities at Hobby Hills."

Domingo Ramirez's squinty eyes narrowed.

"What'd he die of?" His lips barely moved as he talked. "Boredom?" Then he said "Ha. Ha." Not a laugh. Just an unsmiling ejaculation of two syllables.

"There was a fire."

His right eye widened a fraction. "I heard something about a fire. So it was the old guy up the road." This time he did laugh. A single, humorless grunt. "Probably his skirt caught on fire." Another grunt. "Talk about weird." He fixed his eyes on Sebastian. "So. Like I said, what's it got to do with me?"

"I want to know about the day that Morgan Mason came here."

"Nice day. No clouds. No breeze. Lots of sunshine. Nothing to complain about. "

"What did you talk about?"

"Hey. Did you know the old guy was running for mayor?"

"I knew."

"Well, that's what we talked about. A mayor of a town's got to have dignity. I said to him, 'Lose the skirt and I'll vote for you.'"

"What else did you talk about?"

"We didn't talk. We had coffee. Yeah. I gave him some cookies. Chocolate chip cookies and coffee. Real neighborly like."

"Mr. Mason didn't drink coffee," Billy said. "He drank tea."

"My coffee tastes like tea."

"He didn't come here to complain about the loud music or your people leaving garbage on his lawn?"

Domingo Ramirez's small eyes became smaller. He reached for his wallet. "You want a contribution for a funeral bouquet? I'm good for a hundred bucks."

"He annoyed you," Sebastian said. "He was a pest."

This time Ramirez's laugh went on for three full grunts. "You think an old guy like that bothers me? You think I snuck out in the middle of the night and whacked him? Ha! What could he do to me? Nothing, that's what. Nothing. Nada. Zero. ¿Comprende?"

"He drove here in the middle of the day on his tractor," Billy said.

"You call that a tractor? It's a piece of junk."

"And he—"

"Look." Ramirez took a step forward and pointed a stubby finger at my brother's face. "Old men in skirts don't bother me. Cops don't bother me. You don't bother me."

"I'd put that finger down if I were you," Sebastian said in that quietly emphatic way he has that is impossible to ignore.

Ramirez looked at his finger. "Why? It isn't loaded." But he dropped his hand.

"What does bother you, Mr. Ramirez?" Billy persisted. "We don't. Morgan Mason didn't. What does?"

"You want to know? Those jerks in Killdeer who think they can push me around. They bother me."

"Is the town trying to shut you down? Won't they issue you any more permits?"

"I got my permits."

"Then what—"

"I don't have to tell you anything."

Sebastian looked at Billy. Billy looked at Sebastian. Together, they turned and started to walk back to the car.

Ramirez called out after them.

"The tax assessor," he barked. "Tell her something for me."

Sebastian stopped.

"What?"

"Tell her I know who she is."

"Is that a threat, Mr. Ramirez?"

"Not a threat. But maybe someday, like that nosey old farmer, I'll invite her over for a cup of coffee that tastes like tea."

WHEN SEBASTIAN and Billy had finished telling me about their interview at Hobby Hills, I said, "The village assessor is Rose Gimbel. She and I go to the same manicurist. I like her very much. There's something comforting about Rose."

It was a beautiful night. Brilliant stars on a black blanket of sky looked like golden dots on an illuminated manuscript. As I gazed up, I imagined tiny letters under each group identifying them as the Big Dipper, the Little Dipper, Cygnus, Capella, and Cassiopeia.

I had made a pitcher of lemonade and we sat lazily around the picnic table in the backyard.

"Comforting?" Billy said doubtfully. "You make her sound like an old lady."

"Oh, no. Rose isn't old. I'd be surprised if she's even thirty-three."

"Why has Ramirez got it in for her?"

"It's a puzzlement." I drew a smiley face on the sweat coating the lemonade pitcher. "Rose is . . . well, she's like her name."

"Beautiful?"

"No. Pretty. Sweet. Dependable. A country rose. Not a hothouse rose. Very gentle and kind. She was trained as a librarian, and she works for the Four County Library System in the bookmobile. I don't think she's had much of a life. Both of her parents were sick for years. She bought a little house up the street from them and took care of them before and after work. Her mother had a bad heart and her father had Parkinson's disease. They died within a month of each other about two years ago. That's when Rose became the Killdeer village assessor. It's a part-time job. I think she does it because she's lonesome and the library work isn't enough to keep her busy. She's . . ."

I stopped mid-sentence and snapped my fingers. "Why didn't I think of that before?"

"Think of what?"

But I shook my head and temporarily dismissed both the problem and my possible solution.

"Do you know what I like most about Rose Gimbel?" I asked. I didn't wait for an answer. "She's a cross between Mom's apple pie and a Shakespeare sonnet. There's something about her that's both down home and lyrical."

Billy tapped an impatient finger against the top of the picnic table.

"Which has exactly what to do with our investigation?"

"I'm not sure." I turned to my husband. "But is it all right if I follow up on the Rose angle?"

"Suit yourself," Sebastian said. "Since there isn't one. If she had been found dead in a fire, that would be a connection. But the Skirt Man is dead, not your friend; so follow up to your heart's content."

I got up and gave my husband a kiss on the cheek.

"You are so nice," I said fondly. "Other husbands give

their wives jewelry. You give yours the go-ahead to poke into other people's lives."

Sebastian grabbed me by the wrist and pulled me down onto his lap.

"You'd do it anyway, wouldn't you?"

I laughed.

"There is that remote possibility."

chapter 14

THE INVESTIGATION proceeded.

Sebastian contacted Creedmore Snowdon at his television station in New York City, and much to everybody's surprise, the producer quickly volunteered the videotape that he had taken the night of the Skirt Man's death.

"My dear boy, of course you don't need a subpoena." His attitude was suspiciously accommodating. "We are all good friends in Killdeer."

Creedmore promised to overnight the tape to Troop C Headquarters in Sidney, New York. Then he went on, preening like a peacock, "You did see the show, didn't you? One of my best efforts, I think, the way I tied that poor farmer's death to the elements of spontaneous human combustion."

He continued to prattle on, cheerfully self-absorbed, thoroughly convinced he had been a good little Boy Scout in assisting the local police, and utterly unaware that Sebastian wanted to throttle him for obstructing justice and contaminating the crime scene.

The videotape arrived at 9:30 on Tuesday morning. Forensics spent the next few hours comparing the twelve minutes of footage Creedmore had taken—mostly outtakes that had not been broadcast on *Heaven and Earth*—with the fifteen-minute video the state police photographer had shot at the scene.

The general consensus, with which Sebastian agreed, was that other than leaving behind footprints, the television producer had removed nothing from the Skirt Man's house and had brought nothing to it.

My brother did not disagree with their conclusions, but he wasn't ready to dismiss the relevance of Creedmore Snowdon's videotape that quickly, either.

BILLY LIVED, BREATHED, dreamed, and schemed fire. Where someone else might see only a fire-damaged wall, Billy Nightingale could see the V pattern between two wall studs where the paneling had been severely burned around an electrical outlet, and he could point out where the burning had become less severe as it rose higher on the wall away from the point of origin.

"It's like this," he once explained to me. "You tell a cop that someone was murdered in a house fire and his natural inclination is to rush through the structure and locate the body so that he can rush off somewhere else, develop leads, and make an arrest. A fire marshal's approach to the scene is completely different. First he assesses the exterior of the premises. Then he proceeds inside, room by room, burn pattern by burn pattern. He's slower. More methodical. Because he knows that hidden in that fire scene is the solution to the crime."

And so Billy asked for and was given a copy of Creedmore's videotape, and he asked for and received permission to go back to the Skirt Man's house. But before he went there, he stopped at our house in Fawn Creek to borrow our portable television set—the one with a built-in VCR. I gave it to him, along with a twenty-foot extension cord.

"Those old farmhouses sometimes only have one outlet per room," I said. Then I followed Billy to the car, opened the passenger door, and got in.

He looked at me.

"Someone's got to carry the extension cord," I explained.

Billy grinned. I grinned back.

We get along well, my brother and I. We are both completely dedicated to justice and more or less committed to the concept of doing right.

Billy more so, because he does it professionally.

Me less so, because I do everything less.

One evening when we were kids back in Wyoming, we were watching an old British film on TV called *The Winslow Boy*, which was based on a play by Terrence Rattigan. The story was about a schoolboy falsely accused of stealing a money order. His father and sister appeal the ruling all the way up to whatever the British equivalent is to our Supreme Court. At the end of a grueling and valiant legal battle, the boy's attorney, played to perfection by Robert Donat, demands of the court, "Let right be done."

This is what Billy and I care about. That right be done.

We do not, however, have terribly big commitments to the truth, as my husband has often commented upon with regret. Which is why Billy let me out of the car about twelve hundred feet north of the Skirt Man's house so I could sneak in from behind the barn while he openly carried our television set through the side door.

"If you want to go to town and grab a bite to eat," I heard him tell the state trooper guarding the scene, "I'll keep an eye on the place until you get back. Take your time. I'll be here for at least an hour."

I waited until I heard the trooper's car pulling out of the driveway. Then I crept into Morgan Mason's house and watched my brother go to work.

He hooked the extension cord to an outlet in the kitchen, positioned the VCR on the floor in the hallway at the opening to Morgan Mason's living room, and loaded the cassette.

Once he was set up, Billy stretched out, his elbows on the floor, his chin resting on the knuckles of one hand. He pressed the PLAY button, and his eyes flicked back and forth as he compared the Skirt Man's living room—the way it had looked when Creedmore Snowdon videotaped it—with the way the living room looked now.

When Billy had first shown me the grisly crime-scene photographs, my focus had been on the fire-gutted chair and the no-longer-human remains of the man who had been sitting in it. But here, at the actual fire scene, my focus switched to the man himself.

Who was Morgan Mason? Did he have a secret life?

How had he lived? How had he died?

I looked around his living room. It was sparsely furnished. There was a Ben Franklin stove in the middle of the room. The old sofa that Sonny and Moe Dillenbeck had described as being covered with ugly brown tweed was, indeed, old, but the worst thing you could say about it was that it looked like every sofa in every 1950s era den. The cushions, not too woefully deflated by the march of posteriors over the decades, had been further darkened by a layer of soot.

There were framed Charles Russell prints on three of the room's walls: a cowboy and his horse at a campfire, a buffalo hunt, and a bunch of wranglers huddled on their horses in a snowstorm. As a Wyoming girl, I had seen all of these prints dozens of times before. It wasn't often, though, that I came upon them east of the Mississippi River.

I continued to inventory the room. Other than the sofa and framed prints, there were a footstool, which Billy thought the arsonist might have deliberately pushed away from the Skirt Man's chair; a small side table standing about three feet from where the chair had been; a radiator; and hip-high bookshelves against each wall.

I was dying to wander inside and find out what books Morgan Mason had read, but I didn't dare get between Billy and his field of vision as he studied the room. He seemed particularly interested in the wide plank flooring; it had settled over the years and was not as tight as it once had been. There were gaps between the tongues and the grooves, the baseboards didn't quite meet the floorboards, and the corners of the baseboard trim were askew.

"What are you doing now, Billy?"

I knew that he was checking Creedmore's video against what was still in the room, but I was a bit foggy as to what exactly that entailed.

"I'm looking for anything—a scrap of paper, a revolver, a bottle cap, a lug wrench—something that was here when Snowdon videotaped the room but was gone by the time Sebastian and I got here. Something that could have been removed or dislodged. Maybe as small as a rubber band or a thumbtack."

Billy alternately depressed the PLAY and PAUSE buttons on the small television set, continually interrupting the panning motion of Creedmore Snowdon's camera.

The base of a bookshelf. *Start. Stop.*

A scattering of charred wood where the chair had stood. *Start. Stop.*

The corner of the room behind the chair. *Start. Stop.*

The slab of slate underneath the wood stove. *Start. Stop.*

I got up from the floor and wandered off to explore the rest of the house, silently promising myself, as Sonny had promised Sebastian, *Don't worry, Mr. State Trooper, sir. I won't touch anything.*

Not that there was a whole lot to touch.

The Skirt Man had been a good housekeeper, but there was something so forlorn and lonely about the place that I could have cried.

The room next to the living room was used as an office. In it were an old oak desk and a wooden swivel chair, with a small filing cabinet beside the desk where Morgan Mason must have paid his bills and maintained his farm records.

A narrow staircase led from there to an attic.

Across the hall was the Skirt Man's bedroom, with its sad and solitary single bed, a night table bearing a cheap ceramic lamp, a straight chair in one corner, a small closet in the other, a chest of drawers against the wall, and a hooked rug in the middle of the room. I nodded gratefully at the rug, thinking, *At least his feet touched something warm when he got up in the middle of the night.*

I was on my way to Morgan Mason's closet because some morbid curiosity drove me to find out how many skirts he had, to touch them, and to see what they were made of (I know that I had promised I wouldn't touch anything, but I lied) when Billy called out, "Annie. Come here."

I hastened back to the hallway, dropped down to the floor, and looked at where the tip of his finger was pointing on the television screen.

"What do you make of that?" Billy asked me.

"It looks like a slug," I said, staring at a small, round disk obscured by shadow and partially hidden by one short leg of a radiator. "Or maybe a washer. I can't tell if there's a hole in the center or not. Why? What about it?"

"It wasn't on the videotape the state police took," Billy said. He got up and dusted off his jeans. "Maybe one of the firemen kicked it under a piece of furniture during his search. Maybe Sebastian did. Or I did. Whatever it is, we didn't see it here on Saturday night."

I followed Billy into the living room.

"Maybe it isn't important," I suggested.

"Maybe it is," my brother replied.

He knelt by the radiator. "Look on the other side of the room, Annie. Check the crevices between the floorboards and the wall. Look under the stove. Look under and behind the bookshelves. If you find it, whatever it is, don't—"

"I know the drill," I laughed. "Don't touch it!"

WE SEARCHED every crack and cranny of that room. Having a short attention span, I was ready to quit after five minutes, but Billy's focus never faltered. Ultimately, even though he didn't really find what he was looking for, it more or less found him.

Twenty minutes from when we had started, I looked at my watch, got up off my hands and knees, and started toward the hall.

"That trooper you hustled off to lunch will be back any minute, Billy. I'll wait for you up the road by the satellite dish."

I opened the door to what I would consider a foyer but in a farmhouse would most likely be called a mudroom, not realizing that Billy was right behind me. So when I turned to ask him how much longer he thought he would be, I was going backward, he was going forward, and we crashed into each other. In the process, we also managed to knock off my baseball cap.

"Sorry," Billy said, bending to pick it up. But halfway down, he stopped and stared at an object against the west wall of that small space.

"Annie," he said, his voice electric with anticipation. "Can you think of any reason why I would assume a house this size only had one radiator in it?"

I opened the front door, stepped out on the porch to give him more room, and with an airy wave of my hand said, "Be my guest."

Billy hunkered down to search under the radiator, the base of which was an exact match to the one we had seen in Creedmore Snowdon's video.

"What I don't understand," I said as Billy began to gently sweep the narrow space beneath the radiator with a pencil he had taken from his pocket, "is why anyone would have bothered to videotape this hall."

Billy looked up. "It was probably a thumb shot."

I stared at him blankly.

He smiled. There was no tension in his face now; his eyes were clear and happy. Billy was an investigator. He lived for moments like these.

"A thumb shot," he said, his eyes still on mine instead of on where his pencil was probing, "is the picture you take when you forget that your camera is on. It can be a kneecap, a pair of shoes, a treetop, a ceiling, or, of course, a thumb." His pencil snagged on something, and his blue eyes lit up. They were as pretty a blue as a bouquet of forget-me-nots.

He glanced down, smiled, and said, "Aaahh."

I crouched in that small space beside him and watched intently as, with one last motion of his pencil, the object he had been seeking slid out from under the radiator.

I looked down. Then I looked over at Billy.

"It's a coin," I exclaimed.

He studied it for a minute. Then he said cheerfully, "A 1922 silver dollar, to be exact."

I DIDN'T HAVE TIME to gloat with Billy over his find when I remembered the imminent arrival of the state trooper. I shot out the door, ran behind the barn into the hedgerow, and started to push through the stands of evergreen and hawthorn trees to our meeting place at the satellite dish. I couldn't have walked more than fifty feet before I heard two people talking not far off in the woods. Their voices had been so permanently embedded in my brain by the pygmy goat experience that I didn't even bother to conceal myself as I moved in the direction where I thought they might be.

"Hello, boys," I said pleasantly to Sonny and Moses Dillenbeck.

Moe was looking particularly long, lean, and angular that morning. A few twigs had gotten tangled in his curly hair, and an expression of perplexity drew a shadow over the big features of his pleasant if inelegant face.

He was staring at something on the ground.

Sonny, far more handsome but no less puzzled, was down on one knee and gazing at that same thing.

Both boys turned in unison.

Sonny stood and wiped his hands on his pants.

"Hey there, Mrs. Bly. Seems like you caught us in the act."

I looked to my right and to my left. "Who caught whom might be a subject that warrants discussion, but not now. What have you got there?" I moved forward; Sonny took a step back to clear the way for me. I crouched and saw something nestled in a bed of oak leaves and crabgrass. After three or four seconds, I raised my head.

"A jar?" I asked Sonny and Moe.

"That's what we think," Moe said. He knelt on one side of me and Sonny knelt on the other. We stared down at the white object as if it were the baby Jesus and we were the three wise men.

"What do you think, Mrs. Merry's mother?"

Hell. I hadn't yet absorbed the ramifications of finding the silver dollar let alone this new whatever-it-was not far from the scene of a terrible crime.

"What *you* think is more to the point. When did you find it?"

Sonny looked at Moe. Moe tugged at an earlobe with a pair of huge fingers. "Maybe a minute or two before you got here."

"I suspect this is a case of the pot calling the kettle black," I murmured. "But what are you boys doing here?"

"We were looking for stuff," Moe said, as though the answer should have been obvious.

Sonny got to his feet.

So did Moe.

"We're helping your husband figure out what happened to Mr. Mason."

"We already found Buddy for him. Buddy was behind the barn."

"Dead," Sonny added somberly.

"We figured whoever killed Buddy probably killed our friend."

"And because he'd already left something in the woods, he might have left something else."

My legs were cramping. I also stood up. "I get it," I said, remembering a series of detective books that Billy used to read when my parallel universe had been Nancy Drew. "The Hardy Boys."

Moe took a deep, sad breath.

Sonny sighed.

"We were afraid you would think that."

"Sorry. So, what have you two decided?"

"We haven't yet. We were trying to figure out what to do when you got here. Maybe it's just a jar of sunscreen."

"Or hair goo."

"Or hand cream."

"But it could also be—and don't laugh, Mrs. Bly. But it could be *important*," Moe said.

"Maybe some kind of poisonous ointment the killer applied to Mr. Mason before he set him on fire," Sonny suggested. Then he took a step behind me so that he was standing shoulder to shoulder with his brother. Two against one. Except that I wasn't against them. My Nancy Drew flag was flying at full mast.

"It could be *evidence*," Sonny said, his voice low, his eyes wide with the realization of the burden that finding such a thing would entail.

"So we didn't want to touch it."

I bent down, picked up a convenient twig, and gently pushed aside a leaf that had been obscuring much of the jar. There didn't appear to be a label on the jar, so I let the leaf fall back into place.

"You met my brother the night of the fire. He's inside Mr. Mason's house right now. Why don't you bring him here and show him what you've discovered. He'll know what to do."

Sonny nodded.

Moe nodded.

They started to walk in the direction of the Skirt Man's house. Then Moe stopped and turned back toward me.

"Coming?"

I shook my head. "I'm not really here, Moe."

He looked at me skeptically.

"I'm ... oh ... somewhere nice. Maybe in our barn. Giving Livingston goaty-type things to eat."

He nodded slowly.

"So we didn't see you. Right?"

"Right."

"Does our future father-in-law know that you're here?"

"Not yet. But he will tonight."

Moe blew out a relieved breath. "That's good. We wouldn't want to start out such an important relationship with a lie."

chapter 15

I DON'T KNOW if it's that I live in a strange household or if I am just married to an unusual man.

Unlike most people in law enforcement, Sebastian does not have a secretive nature. If he comes home after a horrendous encounter with a bunch of weapon-wielding miscreants and I ask him how his day was, he actually tells me.

My theory is that if it's ugly and stays inside of him, it can fester. But if he tells me, then he gets rid of it.

Okay. I know what you're thinking. Yeah. Sure. *He* got rid of it, but now *you're* stuck with a truckload of ugliness and grief. It isn't that way at all, though. Because as long as Sebastian has come back to me safely, nothing bothers me in the least.

You see, I have a Teflon psyche.

In. Out.

There are times when it pays to be shallow.

Sebastian and I help each other through things. When I have problems, such as why the hell am I the editor in chief of a newspaper that I'm not even sure I want to work for, Sebastian indulges me, pampers me, pets me, and laughs at me. He laughs because I tend to dramatize things. Truly, my crises, compared to those of people who inhabit the real world, the world he claims that I don't live in, are minuscule indeed.

As Merry has gotten older, Sebastian and I have gradually permitted her to participate more and more in our adult conversations, and except for minor editing—he won't talk about sex crimes or domestic abuse in front of her—he is just as willing to listen to her unsolicited opinions as he is to mine.

Merry's are rarely as useful as they are creative, but that adds to the fun.

Sometimes in the dead of night, when Sebastian and I can't sleep and great attacks of silliness come upon us, we joke that if he had been Clark Kent and I had been Lois Lane, the minute he had realized that I was gazing longingly at the guy in blue tights, he would have told me that he was Superman.

Alas. So it is with me.

Had I been a covert CIA operative (what ever happened to the word "spy"?) and I was told that I had to swear on a Bible that I would never, ever reveal anything I knew about the agency to another living soul, I would blithely place my hand on the Bible, take my oath, and not mean a word of it.

Sebastian is my moral compass.

I am his.

I often wonder if one of the reasons governments don't allow spies to tell their mates what they are doing is simply that governments don't want second opinions.

Think about it.

Your boss says, "Do what I am telling you to do. It is right."

You, however, aren't quite sure. So you go home and toss the idea around with your spouse.

He or she says, "Are you crazy? Not only is it wrong, it's ghastly!"

Thus objectively confirming your own gut instincts.

That is the way it should be.

However, if you are forbidden from consulting *anyone* outside your small, self-contained professional circle, then pesky and bothersome issues like morality can be skimmed over like the small print on a contract.

Not that I would ever have to worry about such things with Sebastian. He is much more moral than I am and our conversations are more along the lines of "Do you think it was an inside job?" or "Had she ever been in jail before?" or "Where does it itch?"

BEFORE BILLY LEFT the Skirt Man's house that afternoon, he photographed the jar the Dillenbeck boys had found in the grass, put it in an evidence bag, labeled the bag, and gave it to the trooper on guard to turn over to the state police forensic unit.

When Billy and I pulled into the driveway of my house in Fawn Creek, Merry was lolling lazily in the hammock in the front yard. Sebastian and I had hung the hammock in that little garden area because it was the only place where two tall, strong trees grew close enough together to provide some shade. But with her coppery hair cascading over one side of the hammock into a bed of lush green ferns, our daughter looked so enchanting that our motive for putting it there could just as easily have been to create a work of art on our front lawn.

I have already boasted and bragged inexcusably about Merry, but I haven't really told you very much about the child. You know that she is a ballet dancer, that she is slim and beautiful, with fair skin and enormous brown eyes; but you don't know that her hair shimmers fiery and golden in the sunlight; and you don't know that, despite the application of every conceivable lotion and potion, she has never discovered a way to eliminate the spray of freckles across her nose that she hates and that I think is adorable; and you don't know about the bond between her and my brother.

I am sure that you have heard of the concept of the self-made man.

Well, our pale and frail and fairylike daughter, even as an infant, evidenced an unshakable will that enabled her to survive a potentially lethal home life and become what I like to think of as a self-made orphan.

Sebastian and I adopted her, and she is in every way, shape, and form our daughter.

But Billy found her. Billy saved her. And with Billy she has a special and really quite magical relationship.

He calls her Marmalade because of her bright orange hair.

She calls him "My Uncle Billy," the way an idealistic schoolgirl might say, "My full scholarship to the University of Good, Noble, and Heroic Deeds."

Merry tumbled out of the hammock as we walked across the lawn, and she followed us into the house, demanding to know details about the interview with Domingo Ramirez and asking if we had learned anything from watching Creedmore Snowdon's videotape. Then she added, "Oh, by the way, Mom, you got ten phone calls from various screaming people at the *County Courier and Gazette,* each of which was urgent, and all of which I placed in a pile on your desk."

I left my brother to update Merry on the Skirt Man investigation, and I went into my office to think.

My life, I decided, had become complicated.

I had responsibilities.

I had deadlines.

There were people counting on me to produce a newsworthy publication in which local merchants would want to advertise and that people would want to read.

It was a dilemma.

I did not want to be an editor in chief, but I did not want Slim Cornfield to sell the *Gazette* to a syndicate. If that happened, would FAWN CREEK GIRLS' VOLLEYBALL TEAM WINS STATE CHAMPIONSHIP still be considered worthy of a front-page story? Or would we be inflicted with headlines like APPEALS COURT JUDGE ARRESTED IN BRIBERY SCANDAL?

Up until the night before, I believed that I had only two options.

Refuse to be anointed as editor and bid bye-bye to the *Gazette* as a hometown paper.

Accept the position as editor and relinquish that finger I have always managed to maintain on the pulse of languor.

Either way I would lose, and losing was unacceptable.

Which was why I had to come up with a viable third alternative.

I picked up the telephone and punched in the numbers for Nails by Pamela.

"Pam," I said. "It's Annie."

"Hold on a second," my manicurist responded. "I've got to check my calendar."

I waited.

"Okay. Nine o'clock tomorrow morning. Your usual appointment. Still want it?"

"Will Rose be there?"

"Rose is my 9:15 and Lillian is my 9:30."

"Book me."

I hung up and walked into the living room.

"Merry," I asked. "When do you have to be back in the city?"

My daughter had collapsed into our cushiest armchair.

Her legs were stretched out in front of her, and she flexed her feet. I observed ten cute little toes peeking out of flip-flops. Did they miss their little wads of lambs' wool? Did they ache to be back in ballet slippers leaping across a stage?

I somehow didn't think so. Looking more like an indolent teenager than a prima ballerina, Merry sighed, "I have five delicious days during which I plan to do as much of nothing as possible."

I went over and sat on the arm of her chair.

Merry has such a pretty nose. It is small and sculpted and it fits her face perfectly. I dropped a finger down and tapped its freckled tip.

Merry laughed, pushed my hand away, and said, "Oh, I almost forgot to tell you. Sonny and Moe are taking me to Hobby Hills on Friday night."

I leaped to my feet and instantly locked eyes with my brother.

"Uncle Billy already knows," Billy said. Not only did he not look worried, he seemed to be on the veritable cusp of a chuckle. I could have murdered him right then and there.

I swiveled angrily back to Merry. "Why would those two idiots take you to that den of iniquity?" I demanded.

"Idiots? I thought you liked them."

"I do. I did. I don't," I sputtered.

Merry stood and began to pat me gently on the head. "Nice mother."

"They are going to get you killed," I complained. "They probably think Domingo Ramirez murdered the Skirt Man, and they're involving you in—"

Merry tapped the arm of her chair.

"Sit," she said decisively.

I sat. I appealed to Billy.

"You're her uncle. *Do* something."

Billy laughed and said, "Listen to Marmalade."

I sighed.

"Okay." I glared at Merry. "Go ahead. Break your mother's heart. I'm listening."

My face at that moment must have been a pretty poor exaggeration of the mask of tragedy. I admit that I do not have either the physiognomy or the haircut to pull tragedy off. That may be the reason why Merry started to laugh. It was her laughter that brought the reality of the situation home to me. After all, I had spent most of the afternoon sneaking past crime-scene tape and consorting in the woods with the same two boys with whom she was planning to do pretty much the same thing.

So what the hell. I started to laugh, too.

Between gasps of jocularity, though, I did manage to put my hands around Merry's neck and demand, "Promise me that you will be careful or you are a dead dancer."

Which made her laugh all the harder.

And that was how Sebastian found his wife, daughter, and brother-in-law when he walked into the living room carrying two autopsy reports in his hands.

chapter 16

DR. ARISTOTLE PAPPAS had performed the autopsy on Morgan Mason in the basement laboratory of Binghamton Hospital's morgue.

The canine autopsy was done by Dr. Judith Mendola, a pathologist who specializes in veterinary medicine at Cornell University, where, at Sebastian's request, a state trooper had brought Morgan Mason's dog.

Neither report had an O. Henry surprise ending, but both served to propel the case forward in minor if not major ways.

Since Buddy had not been exposed to fire, his body was still intact except at the contact point where he had received a blow to his head. Therefore, the forensic pathologist who did the postmortem was able to be quite specific. Dr. Mendola believed that the implement used to attack the dog had been a crowbar and that the killer had slammed the claw end of the tool into the left side of Buddy's head.

Based on the width of the wound, which was just under an inch and three-quarters, she also believed that the crowbar had been anywhere from 30 to 48 inches in length and that it weighed five to eleven pounds.

So conscientious was Dr. Mendola in her evaluation that she sketched her idea of what the claw end would have looked like and included the dimensions of the V-shaped notch.

If her assumption was correct, the assailant (her word) would not have needed to be very large, very powerful, or very strong, since the weight of the crowbar and its momentum as it swung toward the dog's head could have provided more than enough force to break the bone in Buddy's skull.

She added that if the claw had been part of a smaller, lighter, and shorter implement, then the attacker would have had to be correspondingly stronger to wield the same force.

Either way Dr. Mendola was certain about the dimensions of the claw and that a claw found on the end of a typical crowbar had been used as the weapon.

Earlier in the day, Sebastian had asked Dr. Mendola to fax her report to Dr. Pappas at Binghamton Hospital so that he could have her assessment of the weapon used on Buddy at hand when he performed the autopsy on Morgan Mason.

Dr. Pappas, of course, had a much more difficult job since he had to examine a body that had been subjected to intense heat and flames. He could get no carbon monoxide readings because most of the tissue had been burned off the corpse, so he was unable to determine if the Skirt Man had been dead or alive at the time of the fire. A full-body X-ray showed that there were no broken bones below the neck and no bullets—or what Dr. Pappas liked to call "projectiles"—anywhere in the corpse.

The autopsy didn't help much with the time of death, but a motorist on his way into Killdeer that Saturday night had reported to the state police that he had seen Morgan Mason driving his tractor toward his barn at about 7:20 PM. If the Skirt Man had been alive then but dead at 9:55 PM when Creedmore had said that he discovered the body (if Creedmore was telling the truth), the time of death would have to have been between 7:20 PM and 9:55 PM.

Dr. Pappas's examination further confirmed what Billy had pointed out to me in the photos—that the heat of the fire had caused a blowout fracture of Morgan Mason's skull. The exam also revealed a crack at the base of the skull where the skull meets the spinal column. This fracture was not heat induced, but had been brought about by blunt force trauma sufficient, Dr. Pappas was certain, to have been the cause of death.

Dr. Pappas compared the measurements of the cracked bone at the base of the skull with the dimensions Dr. Judith Mendola had postulated for the crowbar claw. He concluded that such a tool could, indeed, have created the injury that he observed on Morgan Mason's body, but that the fire damage to the surrounding tissue and bone was so severe he could not exclude any other type of implement.

Not written in the autopsy report was a comment the forensic pathologist made to Sebastian as the two men were walking out of the laboratory.

"One motive for arson," Dr. Pappas said, "is to destroy evidence of the commission of another crime. What we have here is as close to a textbook case of that phenomenon as we are ever going to get."

chapter 17

I HAVE SPENT more time with one manicurist than most women spend with one man.

When I first met Pam, her name was Pamela Sabella and she was a checkout clerk at the Bargain Rite Grocery Store in Fawn Creek. Her platinum blonde hair, tight jeans, gold navel ring, and full battle-dress makeup were small clues that she wasn't born in Fawn Creek. The bigger clue by far was her Brooklyn accent.

"Hey, Mrs. Brody. I see you are buying toilet paper again. Why don't you go back to aisle three and get another four-pack? They're two for the price of one today."

Pam was as cheerful behind the cash register as she was noticeable.

"Mr. Buckspan. Mr. Buckspan. Mr. Buckspan. You forgot again that you're allergic to dairy products. Wait here a minute and I'll get you the yellow box with the fake cheese."

I got such a kick out of Pam Sabella's good-natured friendliness that if there was no line behind me when I was making my purchases, I took to asking her about herself.

I am, I admit, incurably nosy, and she was about as incon-
spicuous as a chorus girl doing high kicks in the Vatican.

Her parents, it turned out, had immigrated to the United
States from Italy. When she was born, they were living on
Eighteenth Avenue in Brooklyn, about three blocks from the
elevated subway line. Her first language had been Italian, but
she confessed regretfully that she had forgotten all of her Italian verbs.

"All I can remember," she laughed, "is how to ask for food."

She was twenty-seven years old when she had moved to
Fawn Creek. She came here after her allegedly future husband jilted her on her wedding day.

"He was such a schmuck," she said, exposing her true
command of what New Yorkers consider to be English. "And
I couldn't stand the commotion afterward. All the relatives
yelling at me in Italian. So I wiped out my checking account
except for a few hundred dollars and told my mother, 'Take
this, Ma, and pay for the wedding. I'm outta here.'

"I went down to the Port Authority Bus Terminal and
looked at the crowds. What I did was to go up to each group
and ask if anyone could change a dollar bill for the pay
phone. Most of them couldn't be bothered and wouldn't
even look in their wallets. But there was this one group of
cheerful looking older people. They didn't have four quarters
between them. But one of them, a little old lady named Mary,
dug into her purse and came out with a bunch of coins that
equaled seventy-five cents. She pushed them into my hand.
When I tried to give her the dollar, she said, 'Don't be silly,
dear. Now, go and make your phone call. We'll keep your
place in line for you.'

"So I found out where that bus was going and where
those people lived, bought a ticket, followed them to Fawn
Creek, and I've been living here ever since."

When I met her, the "ever since" had amounted to only three weeks. At that time, she was renting a furnished room over the Fawn Creek Diner, which my brother Billy rather snobbishly describes as "a dive where they put gravy on everything—even the ice cream."

Back in the city, Pamela Sabella had been a bookkeeper. But she didn't want to do that anymore because "I like people, and numbers don't talk."

Not long after we had become friendly, I was in her checkout line when she looked down at my hands and said, "They're pretty. Why don't you do your nails?"

I answered that I had been too busy lately.

She bagged my groceries, watched me walk away, and as I was pushing my cart through the door, called out that she was coming to my house after work to give me a manicure.

She didn't ask, mind you. She told me.

Suffice it to say, I was worried about what she would do to me since Pam's nails were over half an inch long and resembled billboards displaying American flags, exploding stars, and once what I was certain was a tiny reproduction of Salvador Dali's melting clock.

She was quite artistic.

And very scary.

She came to our house that evening—I think Merry was around four years old at the time—with a full tray of all those things nail ladies carry, even though she was by no means a professional.

"It's my hobby," she explained.

Half an hour later, after she had finished my fingers, Pam laughed and said, "I bet you thought I was going to make you look like a Seventh Avenue whore."

Then she started in on my toes.

She had picked a pale, almost invisible shade of beige,

shaped my nails in the oval that I prefer over the blunt cut then in vogue, and gave me the best manicure and pedicure I had ever had. She refused to take a penny for what she had done. "Hell, Annie. I forced myself on you. Anyway, it was fun." Then she bounced out the door looking extremely pleased with herself.

That was how it started.

I was so impressed by Pam's good taste and sensitivity to the style of the person she was working on that Sebastian and I lent her money to take a cosmetology course at Broome Community College. She returned the money to us within eight months, with interest, and insisted that I be her first official client when she opened Nails by Pamela in the windowless room she had rented behind Earl's Barbershop.

As the years progressed, Pam's business grew, her platinum hair turned a nice shade of ash blonde, and six or seven layers of makeup disappeared to reveal smooth skin, a honey complexion, and ironic eyes. Her nails came to look less like billboards, but were always well groomed and seasonal. They displayed snowflakes at Christmas, pumpkins at Halloween, and stars and stripes on the Fourth of July.

Her client base increased.

She moved Nails by Pamela across the street from the barbershop and hired another manicurist. Then, she surprised us all by marrying Gerry Gilbert, a very nice widower with grown children who drove a truck for Norman Rudd's gravel company. Gerry, you may remember, was also the assistant chief of the Killdeer Volunteer Fire Department.

But Pam never took the gold ring out of her navel. "Some things," she clarified for me, "are sacred."

When Pam and Gerry moved to Killdeer about a year before Morgan Mason's death, they bought a house with a small building in the back. The previous owner had used it as a picture-framing shop. Pam turned it into her nail salon.

Although she usually had one or more freelance manicurists working for her, I never went to anyone but Pam. She was a great listener and a great source of information. On a selective basis, she would pass on tidbits of what she knew to those she deemed worthy.

She was by no means a gossip.

Pam told *me* everything, though.

Or, as she explained it, "If it weren't for you, I'd still be selling pineapple chunks at Bargain Rite. I'm Italian, Annie. I don't forget anything. I've got my code."

I was counting on that code when I surrendered my hands to a bowl of soapy water at nine o'clock on Wednesday morning.

I leaned forward and asked confidentially, "What's going on with Rose Gimbel?"

"She'll be here in a few minutes," Pam answered. "Why?"

"Can you think of any reason why Domingo Ramirez would have it in for her?"

Pam stopped massaging my fingers for a thoughtful few seconds. Then she started up again. "Maybe she turned him down for a date."

I shook my head.

"He came in here once," Pam went on. "Said he wanted a manicure. I said to him, 'I don't do men.' He said, 'Start now and it'll double your business.' I said it was my fondest wish in life to be an underachiever. He gave me a weird kind of ha-ha laugh and left. Frankly, Annie, I can't picture that creep in the same room as Rose, let alone him having—what did you say?"

"That he had it in for her."

Pam frowned.

She said, "I'll ask around," just as the subject of our conversation walked in looking as clean and fresh and all-out nice as she always did.

Rose has dark auburn hair, which she wears in a neat French twist with one little spit curl over each ear. Her nose is a tiny bit too big, but she has a lovely swan neck that cancels out her nose and brings the planes of her face in for a safe landing.

I smiled as she took the seat we all take when we are waiting for our turn with Pam.

"Rose," I said warmly. "I need your brain."

Rose pulled the chair over so that I could see her without having to crane my neck.

"Me, Annie? Whatever for?"

"The Skirt Man."

"You mean Morgan Mason?"

I nodded. "Sebastian is investigating his death."

"Oh." She pulled the chair closer. "How interesting."

"What did you think of Creedmore's show on spontaneous human combustion?" I asked.

Rose grimaced. "I thought it was outrageous."

Pam dried my hand, one finger at a time. "Me, too," she volunteered. "Even though nobody asked *me*."

Rose leaned forward. "How can I help you, Annie?"

I looked into Rose's eyes. Plain eyes. A neither-here-nor-there color, but animated by genuine kindness. I asked, "Did Morgan Mason ever take books out of the library?"

Rose smiled, relieved to be on familiar territory.

"Oh, yes, Annie. All the time. He never missed a bookmobile."

Rose told me that the bookmobile was based out of Binghamton and traveled to all four counties within the library system. On Mondays, it was stocked with books at the head-

quarters behind Vestal Plaza on Club House Road. Its route
took it to the intersections of Route 39 and Route 28 at 12 noon
on the first Thursday of each month.

"Did he often miss the connection?" I asked. "I mean, did
he ever get there after the bookmobile had gone?"

"No. Never."

"Who helped him pick out books?"

"I did. Each bookmobile has a driver, a clerk, and a librarian."

"And you're the librarian."

Rose smiled. "Morgan Mason was very shy, you know."

"So I've heard."

"But there was also a courtliness about him. He was very
respectful. He would follow the bookmobile into the driveway of the town hall—that's where we would make our
stop—then he would get off his tractor and wait until we
were ready to open the door. He stood as straight as a telephone pole with his dog at his side, almost as if they were
both at attention. But . . ." Rose hesitated a moment, her brow
creasing as she sought out a recollection. "I really believe that
in the seven or eight years that I knew him, he only said five
words to me." She smiled again. "'Good morning. Westerns.
Thank you.' Of course he stuttered so badly even that was a
Herculean effort on his part. Why do you want to know,
Annie?"

"I'm trying to get a sense of him. What he liked. What he
was like. What he liked to read."

I didn't admit that I was prying into her life as well.

Rose leaned back in her chair.

Pam applied an undercoat of polish to my right hand.

"Westerns," Rose said. "Morgan loved westerns. Western
novels. Western poetry. I brought him twenty books a month
and he'd zip right through them. Zane Grey. Jack London.

Owen Wister. Bret Hart. Louis L'Amour, Jack Schaeffer, Larry McMurtry. He read so many. I tried to keep track so that I didn't give him the same book twice." She laughed. A low, gentle sound, like a rustle of leaves. "Sometimes I did give him the same books more than once, but he never complained. I think he reread them with the same gusto he had the first time."

Pam pushed my right hand away and reached for my left.

"What was he like?" I asked.

Rose didn't say anything for about fifteen seconds. Then she repeated, "Good morning. Westerns. Thank you." Her mouth curved downward with a sad little twist. "That's what he was like. I think he was a lonely man. I'm sure that he was strong. Both in body and character. His choice of books suggests that he got pleasure from reading about man against nature. Good against evil. And, of course, he was solitary. Like the men he read about." Rose shrugged. "That's all I know, Annie. It's not very much. I'm sorry."

Pam took back my right hand and then my left for the two final coats.

"No. Don't apologize, Rose. What you told me helps."

I decided to move in obliquely for the nitty-gritty.

"Did he pay his taxes on time?" I asked, segueing not too gracefully from her job as a bookmobile librarian to her position as Killdeer village assessor.

"Always."

"Did he complain about his taxes?"

"Never."

"How about Domingo Ramirez?"

Thump. There goes the sandbag.

Rose sat up abruptly.

"What?" The word shot out like a bullet.

"I said, 'How about Domingo Ramirez?'"

She dropped her eyes. "What about him?"

"Did *he* ever complain about his taxes?"

Rose got to her feet.

"I am not the Killdeer tax assessor anymore," she said in a voice so low it was like the whisper of a conspiratorial mouse.

This time *I* shot out, "What?"

But Rose did not repeat what she had said. Instead, she turned abruptly, mumbled, "I'll be right back," and disappeared toward the back of the shop.

When we heard the bathroom door close, Pam slapped me not too gently on the back of my hand, being careful, of course, not to smear my nail polish.

"Annie," she said, "you are an . . . interesting woman. I was going to say 'nice,' but I'm not sure that you *are* nice. And you have as much tact as a battering ram."

She grabbed me by the elbow, pulled me toward a chair as far from her nail station as she could get me, and positioned my fingers under one of those blowy machines that dry nails.

"That's enough harassment for one day," she snapped. She turned on the machine. "Keep it up and I won't have any customers left."

We heard the bathroom door open.

I said to Pam, "Your belly button ring vibrates when you're mad."

She lifted an angry finger to her lips and hissed, "Leave the interrogations to me," just as the door from the street opened and Lillian Roadigger walked in.

I had not seen Lillian since Sunday and assumed that by now her headache would be only a bad memory. Frankly, she didn't look any better.

She was perfectly groomed, as always. Her curly blond hair was neatly combed, and a pair of perky pearl earrings nestled attractively in her ears. Her makeup was just right. But her face was drawn and pale.

I thought back to the magnetic presence she had projected on the stage of the Killdeer High School auditorium, and I couldn't reconcile the two.

Butterfly Saturday night.

Cocoon on Wednesday.

Butterfly. Cocoon. Butterfly. Cocoon.

Then I remembered a reunion that Billy had taken me to years ago when we both lived in Manhattan and he was a probationary fireman.

Billy had been assigned to Ladder 105 in Brooklyn, a busy firehouse that often had dozens of runs in a single day back when rioters were trying to burn down the city in the 1970s. It was a prestigious place to work. A "fireman's firehouse" to which, it was whispered, one could not get appointed unless he was both Irish and an ex-Marine. Billy was neither, but that hadn't stopped him.

Despite Billy's youth, inexperience, and relative newness on the scene, his captain took a liking to Billy and invited him to one of the exclusive 105 reunions.

I was his date that night.

Neither of us had a clue what we were in for.

The party was held in the recreation room over a volunteer firehouse on Long Island, and the only people who attended, other than me, Billy, his captain, and his lieutenant, were old-timers—hero-relics from another day, still alive but not kicking anymore. They sat slumped in their chairs next to their wives, not speaking unless spoken to. Short men packing too many pounds. Graying or bald, wearing eyeglasses, moving slowly, with dull eyes.

At best, they looked like a group of retired accountants.

Or they did until Billy's captain stood in the center of the room, raised his camera, and shouted, "Group photo!"

Then the most remarkable thing occurred.

My eyes tear up even now when I think about it.

Old men, tired men, used-up men wearily pushed themselves away from their tables. They got to their feet and started to walk toward where the captain was assembling them. And step by step, I could see their shoulders pulling back, their stomachs sucking in, their heads rising, their chins jutting, and their eyes brightening.

Men who had shrunk in height grew six feet tall in the time it took them to walk halfway across the room. Affectionate insults were hurled. Fake punches were traded. I heard chuckles and laughter.

I got up.

Billy got up.

Drawn forward by the irresistible energy coming from that side of the room, we stood behind the captain with his camera, and we stared at the former firefighters of Brooklyn's notorious Ladder 105.

They were magnificent.

At that moment, each one of them could have scaled a wall, ripped down a ceiling, vented a roof, or carried a beautiful blond out of a burning building.

I looked at Billy.

He looked at me.

We both said at the same time, "Wow!"

And that was the only explanation I could think of for the transformation of Lillian Roadigger. Something had occurred prior to the night of the Killdeer Town Hall benefit—something that had caused a woman as tightly bound as a mummy in a museum to rip through her bindings and unfurl a spectacular span of butterfly wings. Maybe it had been the audience. Maybe it was the applause. Maybe it was the opportunity to be the focus of everyone's attention.

Whatever it was, I was certain that it had been as transitory as the lifespan of a mayfly.

Born. Die.

Hello. Good-bye.

"Good morning, Annie," Lillian said as she took the chair next to Pam's station, her voice straining to be pleasant.

Poor butterfly, I thought, echoing the words of an old song.

Then I quietly tucked away my thoughts about our town historian, said my good-byes, and walked out of Nails by Pamela, not knowing that every one of my speculations about Lillian Roadigger would turn out to be wrong.

chapter 18

WHEN I GOT INTO my car, I did not know if Slim Cornfield would be at home; however, I was not going to telephone him first and give him the opportunity to escape.

Pam was right about me.

Sometimes, I'm not very nice.

An idea had come to me that suggested a course of action, which at worst would solve one of my problems and at best would solve the problems of at least two other people.

And so I was on a mission.

I was also in luck, because Slim's car was parked in his driveway. When I tiptoed around to the back of his house, I saw him standing a few feet inside the opened door of his garage, knee deep in gardening equipment.

"Slim!" I called out.

My once and future boss looked up. He didn't smile, and I wasn't all that sure of my welcome until he picked up a broom and threw it at me. Its handle landed on my left foot.

I bent down and picked it up.

Witches fly brooms.

I raised an eyebrow at Slim. "Hey, Boss. Are you trying to tell me something?"

The rake he threw next missed me by two inches.

"I am not your boss," he said. Loudly. Firmly. I like a man with decisive opinions. I took a tentative step forward.

"Are we at war?" I asked.

Slim hurled an old baseball mitt at my feet. I did a quick sidestep. Then I scurried forward and moved into the shadow of the garage.

"I'm cleaning up," Slim said.

I saw a haphazard pile of hoes, edging tools, broken wicker baskets, and empty oil cans strewn in the driveway near where the broom, rake, and baseball mitt had landed.

"I like your style," I said. "Merciless. Emphatic. I thought you would be in Tibet by now."

Slim picked up what looked like a machete and examined it. Then he held it out toward me.

"Want it?"

I studied the implement. The rusty blade had a short handle covered in dust and cobwebs. I lifted my eyes to Slim. He was staring at me. I bit my lip.

"Is this a test?" I asked. "If I say 'Yes,' I get to marry the prince and live in a castle? If I say 'No,' a trapdoor opens under me and I fall into a snake pit?"

Slim shook his head in disgust and threw the machete out of the garage. Evidently, I had failed the test.

"What do you want?" he asked without looking at me.

I shrugged and put a cheerful smile on my face.

"I thought I'd just stop by to see how you're doing."

Slim reached over and plucked a water-warped book off a stack of volumes that all seemed to have suffered a similar fate. He examined the spine and read aloud, "*Agricultural History of New York State from 1930 to 1934.*"

He held this out to me as well, but I had learned my lesson. I took it, opened the book to the first chapter, and read, 'New York State has a varied and well-documented history of crop rotation and experimentation.' I snapped the book shut. "By golly! I've never read anything so out-and-out stimulating in my life. I will cherish this book forever, keep it always beside me on my night table, and—"

Slim snatched it out of my hands and tossed it on the soggy stack from which he had taken it. He was wearing an old pair of jeans, an old pair of tennis shoes, and a torn T-shirt. His sandy brown hair was uncombed and a flop of it fell over one eye, making his ears look less stuck-out than usual.

"You look like a rock star," I said, smiling. Which just goes to show you that my Slim-reading barometer was way off. He stopped what he was doing and dropped his eyes to his wrist, forgetting that he had thrown out his watch the day he had quit. So he reached for my arm, read the time off my watch, and said, "You have five minutes to tell me what you want."

Oh boy.

Retirement had *not* improved his disposition.

"Okay," I said. "Here's the story. I am here to beseech, beg, and implore you to do me a favor. I promise you on a stack of Agricultural Histories of New York that it won't take more than a few hours."

Slim opened his mouth to protest.

"Think it over, Boss," I went on briskly, starting the speech that I had practiced on the way to his house. "If I hadn't agreed to take on your job as editor in chief, you would have had to sell the paper, and what would *that* have involved? Meetings with prospective buyers. Your flying out to talk to them. Their flying in to talk to you. Lawyers. Legal fees. Finder's fees. Commissions. Reading contracts. Revising contracts.

Negotiating employee pensions, layoffs, firings, hirings. End-less phone calls."

"Annie, make your point." Slim's voice was firm. His pleasant eyes brooked no nonsense. I nodded encouragingly. I liked the new Slim.

I took a deep breath.

"My point, by Annie Bly," I announced. But seeing the impatient look in his eyes, I cut the rest of my prepared speech and blurted out, "I am crazy overworked at the *Gazette*, and if I'm going to get the paper out tomorrow, I have to spend all day and probably all night at your...I mean at *my* desk. The story on the Killdeer Town Hall restoration is done, but there's another big story brewing that we've got to cover for next week's edition, and it's going to re-quire some interviews that I don't have time to do."

Before Slim could make the suggestion that I knew he was about to make, I cut him off. "And, no. There isn't any-one else to send. Joan is sick." I lied. "Frank can't write worth a damn, and Trudy is on vacation." I threw Trudy in for the hell of it. We have never had a Trudy working at the *Gazette*.

Slim frowned and started to shake his head.

"Don't *do* that!" I protested. "A man died, and this is im-portant!"

He looked at me sharply. "Who died?"

"The Skirt Man."

"Who or what is a Skirt Man?"

"He was an old farmer who lived on Route 39."

"Dozens of farmers live on Route 39, most of them are old, and a lot of them die. What's so special about this one?"

"He was running for mayor of Killdeer, and he was mur-dered."

Slim's head snapped back ever so slightly, trying but not quite succeeding in suppressing his newsman's instincts.

"We don't do hard news, Annie. Never did."

"We do when it's local, Slim. Always did. You know that. You made the policy."

"What do you want from me?"

"There's a connection between the Skirt Man and—"

"Does this character have a name?"

"Morgan Mason."

"Why do you call him the Skirt Man?"

"He wore a skirt. And don't ask me why, because I don't know. No one knows."

I studied Slim's face. I liked what I saw and I thought I just about had him.

"As I was saying, there is a connection between the Skirt Man, AKA Morgan Mason, and Domingo Nogales Ramirez."

"Death Lake?"

"Exactly. Morgan Mason lived a few thousand feet up the road from Hobby Hills, and he and Ramirez had words. That's what Sebastian tells me."

"The state police are involved in this?"

"It's Sebastian's case."

"So let him investigate. What do you need me for?"

"I need you because Sebastian doesn't believe that there's a connection between Morgan Mason's death, Domingo Ramirez, and Rose."

"Who," Slim glared at me, "is Rose?"

"Rose Gimbel. Killdeer's tax assessor. Ramirez has it in for her. According to Sebastian, Ramirez said, and I quote, 'Tell her I know who she is.'"

The skeptical look on Slim's face softened.

"Sounds very Godfather."

I nodded. "And that's not all. Since Sebastian interviewed Domingo Ramirez—or maybe before, I'm not sure—Rose Gimbel has stopped being the tax assessor."

Slim stared at me.

I went on eagerly. "I tried to find out what the problem was. Had she been fired? Did she quit? But she won't talk to me. And I just don't have the time to do any follow-up. Not if I'm going to get the paper out on time."

I got down on one knee. "Please, Boss. Please. Please."

"I am not your boss."

"Please just do me this one little favor. Go over to Rose's house. Highjack her bookmobile."

"Bookmobile? What are you talking about?"

"Oh, I forgot to tell you. She's also the bookmobile librarian. Call Rose. Kidnap her. Take her out for coffee. I don't care how you do it, but try to find out what the connection is between her, the Skirt Man, and Hobby Hills."

Slim took a step out of the garage. I brushed off my knee and followed him.

"Will you? Will you? Will you?" I pleaded.

He looked down at me and shook his head. But he didn't look stern or stiff or angry, so I knew I had him.

"Annie, you are such a pest."

"Oh thank you! Thank you! Thank you!"

"And if you wrote the way you talk, I would have fired you years ago." He started to walk toward the back door of his house. Then he stopped and asked, "When do you want me to do this?"

"Now. In half an hour. In an hour. I know today is Rose's day off because I just saw her in Killdeer having her nails done."

He opened the door to his kitchen. Slim was a great editor, and he had an unerring instinct for what was news, but he was positively the worst investigative journalist I had ever met. He never knew how to talk to people or how to develop a story. From my point of view, he was absolutely the right man for the job.

I took out a small pad from my purse, scribbled a few lines on the top sheet, tore it off, and handed it to Slim.

"Here's Rose's address and phone number. Home and work. She lives in Killdeer about a block from the park. You'll like her."

"Like her?" Slim said. "I thought she was a murder suspect."

I bobbed my head happily. "Thirty-ish. Pretty. Of course, not as pretty as I am. Efficient. Kind. Sympathetic." I grinned. "Or a clever murderess—possibly a blackmailer mixed up in the death of a farmer and somehow tied to the dealings of our infamous local drug lord."

Slim opened the door to the kitchen. I started to follow him inside.

"Scram," he said. "You've got a newspaper to get out."

I winked at him. "On my way, Boss."

And he closed the door in my face.

chapter 19

BILLY HAD RETURNED to the city to testify at an arson trial in Manhattan so he wasn't along for the three interviews Sebastian did that Wednesday morning. I, of course, was busy putting out the newspaper—not that Sebastian would have let me come along anyway. He *never* lets me break state police protocol. Only at home, when nobody is looking, does he divulge what has gone on during his day.

And it had been a busy one.

Busy and disturbing.

When he told me about his first interview, the one with Lewis Furth, Sebastian had this nail-chewing look on his face. Steel nails, not fingernails. Lewis Furth brought that out in everybody. Pam once had a little run-in with him at the Bargain Rite. Not when she was a checkout clerk but later, when she was shopping there for groceries herself.

She had been in the vegetable aisle, reaching for a bunch of bananas. Just as her fingers were closing around the stem, a thin, hairy hand snatched the bananas out from under her.

She turned, and there was Lewis Furth, smug and sneery, his pronounced Adams apple bobbing up and down like a chicken pecking at bugs in the dirt. Pam, unaccustomed to rudeness in a grocery store, was speechless. She stared at Lewis Furth, appalled.

His face, she said, was sucked in around his mouth like sand around a sinkhole.

"Get your own bunch of bananas," he snarled at her. "These are mine."

A small episode. Trivial. Basically irrelevant. But indicative of how he treated people.

Alf Lubbock, the pizza man at Mario's, had a story about Lewis Furth and a three-quarters-eaten pizza that Lewis had returned, demanding a refund because it had been "uneatable."

He had thrown the box against the counter, leaned forward on his knuckles, and ranted about too many anchovies, too much sauce, and too little cheese, disturbing the diners and causing such a ruckus that, as Alf explained it, "I gave him back the money, just to get rid of him."

Pretty much everyone in town had an unpleasant Lewis Furth story. Margo McCrory over at the bank, whom he had tried unsuccessfully to convince that she had shortchanged him on a hundred-dollar bill. Butch Halsley at the Day and Night, whom Lewis had scalded with hot coffee he pretended to have accidentally spilled on Butch after the counterman realized that Lewis was punching holes in the "free cup" card himself. Stanley Dickens, our rural postal delivery guy, who almost had a heart attack when Lewis put a live snake in his mailbox to punish Stanley for not having delivered a package that Stanley swore nobody ever sent.

The general consensus on Lewis Furth is that he is a devious bastard. Pam's analysis of him is the best. She says that he is the kind of a man who would cut off his thumb so that he could stick it in a bowl of chili and sue the restaurant for serving him contaminated food.

Lewis was always writing hysterical letters to the editor about the street signs on Main Street being too small, the animal leash laws being too strict, the highway department having illegally cut down his favorite tree, turkey hunting season being too long, or deer season being too short. All of which I immediately consigned to the wastebasket.

Lewis Furth was of medium height—maybe five feet nine or ten inches tall. His head was oblong with a receding hairline that gave him an odd little island of hair at the top of his high forehead. He had a narrow, almost lipless mouth; abbreviated eyebrows over hostile, unblinking eyes; and a neck that was too thick for his slim and well-proportioned frame.

His skin was pale and white, like a slug's.

Other than the pallor, hairy knuckles, and pronounced Adams apple, there was nothing particularly horrendous about Lewis Furth's appearance. Nevertheless, the overall effect was repellent.

By day, he brought his warm personality and infectious charm to the Department of Motor Vehicles, no doubt sending license applicants on their way with a newfound intent to foreswear automobiles altogether. After work he would go home to cut holes in his neighbors' fences so that his cattle could graze in their fields.

An all-around nice guy.

It was about 7:30 in the morning when Sebastian knocked on Lewis Furth's door. He continued to knock for another three minutes before Lewis finally staggered into the kitchen wearing a tatty bathrobe and slippers. His hair was sleep-tousled and he was pressing a clump of tissues to his nose.

I should note here that, although Sebastian is an investigator for the Bureau of Criminal Investigation, he does not wear a uniform. However, let's face it. Sebastian looks like a cop.

Lewis Furth opened the kitchen door.

Sebastian's eyes traveled from Lewis's robe to his face.

"No work today?" he asked.

"None of your business." Lewis's voice was gravelly and nasal. "I have a cold. What do you want?"

Sebastian held up his ID.

"Investigator Bly with the New York State Police. I'm looking into the death of Morgan Mason. I want to ask you a few questions. Can I come inside?"

Lewis Furth lowered the tissues from his nose. His brow furrowed and he scowled.

"I don't invite the Gestapo inside my house."

He tried to shut the door.

Sebastian's foot on the threshold kept it open.

"I am a sick man. This is harassment."

"No, Mr. Furth. This is a police investigation. Maybe you would rather come down with me to—"

"Okay. Okay. Keep your truncheon in your pants. First name: Lewis. Last name: Furth. Like mirth, with an FU. Age: Thirty-nine. Occupation: Clerk for the Department of Motor Vehicles. Residence: We're in it. I bought this farm fifteen years ago. Relationship with Morgan Mason: I've never spoken to him, except when he was trying to steal my cows. He was crazy. His dog was crazy. Answer to the question you haven't asked yet: No, I did not kill him. What else do you want to know?"

"Where were you on Saturday from 5 P.M. to around midnight?"

Lewis Furth sneezed.

Sebastian didn't say, "God bless you."

"Is that when the old fart died? You mean I need an alibi?"

"I mean where were you after 5 P.M. on Saturday night."

Lewis leaned back his head, closed his eyes, opened his mouth, and appeared to be thinking. Then his eyes slowly re-opened. "Saturday night. Early show at the Colonia Theater in Norwich. I had a pizza before the movie at that Italian dump across the street."

"What time did the show let out?"

"I don't know. Maybe nine."

"Were you alone?"

"No. I was with the president of the United States. He's like a brother."

"Were you alone?" Sebastian repeated expressionlessly.

"Yeah. Me and about forty other people."

"What movie did you see?"

"Something about drugs and Vegas. It was a lousy movie. I don't remember the name."

"When did you get home?"

"Half an hour more or less after the show let out."

"Can anyone verify that you were in the movie theatre?"

"Sure. Talk to my buddy, the president of the United States."

Sebastian repeated, a steely edge to his voice, "Can any-one verify—"

"Yeah, yeah. I heard you the first time. Ask the other forty people in the audience. They'll verify I was there."

"Did you see anyone suspicious in the area of Morgan Mason's house on Saturday night?"

"You can't see his house from my property."

"How about from your car on your way to or from the movie?"

"The Colonia is north of here. Mason's house is south. I didn't pass it either way."

"Do you know of anyone who would have a reason to kill Morgan Mason?"

Lewis opened his mouth to answer, but sneezed instead. "No. Nobody," he finally answered. Then he took a backward step into his kitchen and said, "Either arrest me now, or I'm going to bed."

SEBASTIAN'S SECOND interview that Wednesday took place at around 10 A.M. in the home of the Skirt Man's sister.

Decidia Skirball was seventy-four years old, tall, slim, and elegant. She had stylishly short hair; a long, immobile face; impenetrable gray eyes; and perfectly manicured arthritic fingers. In the few years since returning to Killdeer, she had come to know Sebastian, not as an investigator for the state police, but as the father of a local celebrity ballerina and the husband of a reporter for the *County Courier and Gazette*.

Although I did not like her, there was a studied graciousness about Decidia that worked well with her self-image as a chatelaine of the countryside. As such, she relentlessly cultivated social contacts with the cool self-possession of a laboratory technician germinating deadly viruses. And, in her capacity as manager of Creedmore Snowdon's mayoralty campaign, she never turned down the opportunity to give an interview. Not even to the state police.

Decidia greeted Sebastian with what would probably pass for a smile in the plastic surgery set. She led him from the ornately carved front door of her Victorian mansion to a chintz-covered chair in her living room and offered him coffee, iced tea, or lemonade. Then, with unfaltering poise, she talked without being prompted, answered all of the questions Sebastian asked, and didn't really communicate much of anything.

"Yes, Morgan was my brother, but we were never close. My parents left the farmhouse, the lake, and over two hundred acres to him. They left me seventy-five acres with less than fifty feet of road frontage. That's right. Not fair at all. But Morgan was always their favorite. Yes, as the next of kin, I will inherit everything if no will is found. No, Morgan never wanted to be anything but a farmer. I was the ambitious one. Yes, a full scholarship to NYU. That's right; Morgan and I lost touch with each other for over forty years. Utterly ludicrous that he should be running for mayor. Those Dillenbeck boys put him up to it. Domingo who? No, I never heard of him. Hobby Hills? I'm not quite up on that. Absolutely no family sense. None. And when my son tried to befriend him, Morgan was perfectly dreadful. No, no enemies. He didn't seem to be the kind of a man who would have enemies. Not a pal or buddy. No girlfriend either. Just those beastly dogs. As far as I'm concerned, a man wearing a skirt is as silly as a woman walking around in a gorilla suit. Oh dear, you've let your coffee get cold. Perhaps you'd like another? Well then, Investigator Bly, on your way out, *do* let me introduce you to my swans."

Sebastian's attitude toward swans, I should explain, is that they are pigeons with long necks. And pigeons, he insists, are rats with feathers. The antagonism between man and bird must have been mutual because when Sebastian approached, their belligerent squawking rose to such a rapid crescendo that Decidia did not protest when he went directly to his car.

"I'll phone the children," she called after him as he slipped into the driver's seat. "When shall I say that you're going to see them?"

Sebastian gave her a polite wave, pretended not to have

heard the question, and turned out of the driveway, intent on interviewing Decidia Skirball's son and daughter-in-law immediately after he left her house.

"THEY LOOK A little alike," Sebastian told me Wednesday night after we had each tucked away the loose ends of what had been too long of a day. Billy hadn't come back yet from his field trip to the Manhattan criminal courts, but Sebastian had finished his interviews, and I had safely put the *County Courier and Gazette* to bed—if not as competently as Slim Cornfield would have done, at least well enough to keep the threat of a syndicate takeover at bay.

The "they" to whom Sebastian referred were Decidia Skirball and her son, Andrew.

"Both of them have long, narrow faces," Sebastian said. "And wide mouths. But that's where the resemblance ends."

"What's he like?" I asked.

"Good natured, freckle-faced, loose-limbed. You kind of expect him to run into the front yard and come back with a newspaper clenched in his teeth. Big smile. Big face. Friendly. Earnest. Impossible not to like the guy."

We were sitting at the kitchen table. I had been too tired to cook, so we were scooping assorted lumps of green and noodley-looking things from the boxes I had brought back from Wong's Chow on my way home.

"How old is he?" I asked, studying something with a tail and fins that had flopped onto my plate.

"He's forty-one. She's only twenty-six."

"She? What she?" I slipped the finned thing from my plate onto Sebastian's.

"His wife." Sebastian looked at my donation for a dubious

instant and then popped it into his mouth. "Her name is Neverly. They've been married about a year and she's very pregnant."

"Nice." I picked up an egg roll. "What's she like?"

"Cute. Sweet. Crazy about Andrew and visa versa. Neverly was his secretary back in Boston."

"Boston?"

Sebastian dumped the whole carton of finned things onto his plate.

"Andrew was a grade-school principal. Loves children but hates the bureaucracy in public schools. So they moved here. His dream is to open a summer camp for kids. His mother—"

"The widow Screwball?"

"*Skir*ball," Sebastian rolled his eyes at my immature interruption. "She inherited some land when their parents died. Morgan got the lion's share. Farmhouse, lake, and two hundred or so acres. Decidia got seventy-five acres on the wrong side of the creek. After Andrew convinced his mother that he really was leaving Boston to build a summer camp, she gave him her seventy-five acres."

I dipped my egg roll in the duck sauce.

"Nice of her."

"She charged him eighteen hundred dollars an acre."

"*Not* so nice."

Sebastian looked to his right and left.

"What do you want?"

"Where's the tea?"

I got up, filled the kettle, and put it on the stove.

"Tea's coming," I said. "Go on. Nice of her. Not nice of her. Where are we?"

"Somewhere in between. Decidia wanted to give them the land, but Andrew said he knew it wasn't smart to let her give him anything because the price would be too great. I asked what he meant, and he said, 'With Mother, subsidy leads to control.'"

I took the teapot off the shelf.

"After he bought the land from her, then what?"

"Andrew decided to introduce himself to his uncle."

"The Skirt Man?"

"Right. He wanted to meet him because Morgan Mason was his only living male relative and he would be living nearby. Neverly wanted to meet him because she has no family, other than Andrew. They decided to surprise Uncle Morgan with a visit."

I put two tea bags into the teapot and pulled two cups out of the cupboard.

"I sense impending disaster."

Sebastian nodded.

"Neverly had baked a pie and Andrew had built a birdhouse. They brought their gifts for Uncle Morgan on a getting-to-know-you basis. But when they knocked on his door and told him who they were, the old guy shook his head angrily, said, 'You . . . ca . . . ca . . . can't have m . . . m . . . my farm,' and shut the door in their faces."

The kettle started to whistle.

"Decidia," I said firmly.

"Yep," my husband agreed. "Andrew and Neverly were crushed by the rejection. They went right home—they're renting a place in town. Andrew called his mother and demanded to know what she had done."

"What *had* she done?"

"It took him half an hour to pry it out of her, but she'd called Morgan the day before, told him that although she hadn't challenged it at the time, their parents' will was invalid because she didn't get her fair share, and that unless he agreed to deed over half his farm—the half with the lake on it—to her son Andrew, she was going to take him to court."

I turned off the gas under the kettle, forgot to make the tea, and sat down, staring at Sebastian as though he had told me that Jiminy Cricket dies at the end of *Pinocchio*.

"That's horrible," I whispered.

Neither of us said another word for a few minutes.

"Why are they renting a place in town?" I suddenly asked.

"Andrew hasn't decided yet if it's practical for him to build a lake on his mother's seventy-five acres or whether he should sell the property and buy something with a ready-made lake."

"Why does he need a lake?"

"Camps always have lakes."

I frowned and reached for the won ton soup. "Do you think they killed the Skirt Man for a lake?"

My husband looked me dead in the eye.

"Neverly has bright gold hair, eyes like a bunny rabbit, and a smile that could melt a bolt cutter," he said.

But he wasn't smiling.

I lowered my spoon.

"They don't have an alibi for Saturday night, Sebastian. Do they?"

I knew my husband.

He stabbed at a piece of shrimp with his fork.

"Nope," he said.

chapter 20

PRIOR TO GOING OUT on Thursday to track down what he called "medical leads," Sebastian stopped at the house to pick up Billy, who had returned from the city at eleven o'clock the night before.

My husband also wanted to show me the jar.

Or, as I like to call it, "the infamous jar."

I don't know why I got credit for having found it when it was Sonny and Moses Dillenbeck who discovered it in the woods behind the Skirt Man's house, but for some reason— probably because the goat they gave Merry ate his address book—Sebastian adopted the attitude that I had brought the jar to his attention, and therefore, I had earned the right to be kept in the loop.

Before I was permitted to touch this holy grail of evidence, it had been dusted for fingerprints (there was half a thumbprint on the bottom of the jar, but it didn't match anybody's thumbprint in any file anywhere), and a sample of the contents had been retained for analysis by the forensic laboratory.

Sebastian's theory was that waiting for the guys in the lab

coats to identify what it was might take weeks, and since there were so few pharmacists in the area, he could quickly visit them all, show them the jar, and ask if they recognized where it had come from and who it was for.

It seemed logical for Sebastian and Billy to start with the drugstore in Killdeer, since the Skirt Man went everywhere on his tractor and would probably have filled his prescriptions in the town closest to where he lived. If they didn't hit a home run in Killdeer, next on their list would be the pharmacies in New Bassett, Kipplebrook, Valerie, and Fawn Creek.

Before they set off on their quest, Sebastian showed me the jar.

When Sonny and Moe had pointed it out to me in the woods, all I had seen was a small white container partially concealed by dead leaves and grass. Now, as I held it in my hands, I realized that it was a screw top, eight-ounce, white plastic jar with no label. In size and shape, it was about as big as a small jar of peanut butter.

I unscrewed the lid.

The first thing I noticed was the strong odor. It smelled like Vicks or mentholatum. When I looked inside I saw that it was half-filled with a bright white substance the consistency of custard pudding. I shook the jar and the contents jiggled. I touched the jiggly stuff. It felt creamy.

I put a dab on my finger, held it up to my nose, and was about to rub some of it on my wrist.

Sebastian saw what I was doing, grabbed me by the arm, dragged me over to the sink, and ran water over my hand.

"Are you crazy?" he asked.

I laughed.

He turned off the water and dried my hand with a dish towel. "I have to watch you every minute. You're like a kid who has to put everything in her mouth."

He took back the jar, screwed on the lid, and for a time, that was the last I saw of it.

IT TOOK SEBASTIAN and Billy all day, but eventually they found answers to some of their questions. I give them a lot of credit for perseverance, but I still can't help but think that the Nobel Prize for Evidence Excavation should go to Sonny and Moe.

The first pharmacist they visited, the one in Killdeer, about whom Sebastian had held such high hopes, was pretty much a bust.

"All of our jars are blue or brown," he said.

The New Bassett pharmacist, second on their list, thought that he might be able to identify the contents of the jar by the smell, but he backed down when Sebastian pressed him on specifics. He was sure, however, that he had not made it and that it had not originated in his store.

The Kipplebrook pharmacist told Sebastian and Billy that the cream in the jar had not been packaged by a manufacturer and that it had been hand-concocted by a pharmacist. But she had no idea what it was or who might have made it. And the druggist in Valerie merely looked at the jar disdainfully and handed it back to Sebastian with a contemptuous shake of his head.

It wasn't until Sebastian and Billy approached our very own drugstore that they finally started to get answers. Nigel Petherbridge was a slim, erect, silver-haired gentleman who had lived in Fawn Creek for over forty years but still spoke with a noticeable British accent.

He identified it right away.

"Indeed I do recognize this jar. I use white jars for all of the compound creams I make."

Nigel sniffed the contents.

"No question about it. I made this—let me think for a moment—oh, I'd say easily over six months ago." He set the jar down on the countertop. "How else may I help you?"

Sebastian punched him softly on the arm. "Nice try, Nigel. But we've still got a long way to go."

The pharmacist gave a soft, self-deprecating chuckle. "Sorry, Sebastian." Then he cleared his throat as if he were about to recite a long poem by Tennyson and said, "This is what we call a eutectic mixture."

Billy crossed his arms over his chest and leaned back against a cabinet door. "Clear as mud, pal," he said. "Keep talking."

Nigel Petherbridge reached up and took three jars from a shelf.

"A eutectic mixture is a combination of various chemical compounds that have a lower melting temperature after they have been joined together than they do alone."

"Mud," Billy murmured again, loud enough to elicit a sympathetic smile from the pharmacist.

"It's quite simple, really." Nigel said. "I'll show you."

He unscrewed the lid of an eight-ounce jar similar to the one we had found behind the Skirt Man's house, pushed it off to one side, and then opened a small transparent jar.

"This contains menthol crystals."

He tilted it toward Sebastian and Billy, exposing long, jagged, clear crystals as beautiful as any a collector might keep in an illuminated display case.

Nigel extracted a few of them with a spatula.

"I am going to measure out six grams of these menthol crystals and put them into this mortar," he said, weighing the crystals on a balance scale and then sliding them into a small, thick, glass bowl.

He removed the lid from a large opaque jar and showed Sebastian and Billy the powdery white substance inside.

"These are camphor crystals. I'm sure you recognize the smell."

"Mothballs," Billy said.

"Exactly. You'll notice how these crystals clump together somewhat like—"

"Wet snow?" Sebastian suggested.

"Very good!" Nigel beamed at him.

Once again using the spatula, he measured out six grams of camphor crystals and added them to the mortar.

"Now, this is a pestle," he announced, holding up a stone thingamabob that Sebastian said looked like a baseball bat for elves.

He put the pestle in the bowl and started to smash the two crystals together against the sides of the mortar.

Sebastian and Billy watched.

First the crystals softened.

Then they liquefied completely.

Nigel Petherbridge announced, "A eutectic mixture," and he held out the mortar in exactly the same way that a magician might hold up a fishbowl that had been a top hat only seconds before.

He called out to his assistant.

"Doris. Would you please bring me some cold cream?"

A plump woman with a nice smile and a bad haircut handed him a jar.

"Ponds Cold Cream," the pharmacist observed with approval. "Excellent. Now, gentlemen, I am going to add what we call QS—quantity sufficient—to produce eight ounces of lotion."

He measured in the Ponds and pummeled the mixture

with the pestle. Within seconds the contents of the bowl were a perfect match to the contents of the infamous white jar.

Billy pushed himself away from the cabinet.

"Mr. Wizard," he said, grinning and gesturing a thumbs up.

Nigel Petherbridge chuckled.

"That is precisely what pharmacists used to be and why I was drawn to the profession." He picked up the empty white jar that he had put aside, and he poured the lotion into it. "Part doctor. Part alchemist. Part wizard." He screwed on the lid and handed it to Sebastian. "Sorrowfully, those days are long gone. This eutectic compound cream would cost a customer less than twenty dollars and would last him at least a month; however, few doctors today know how to prescribe such a remedy, and those who do don't want to be bothered. It's easier for them to write out a prescription for a tube that costs ninety dollars made by a pharmaceutical company."

Sebastian tapped the lid of the jar Nigel had just given him.

"What does it do?"

"It's a counterirritant and an anti-inflammatory. It can soothe burning sensations and desensitize itchy or irritated skin."

"Who uses it?"

"For this particular composition, not very many people," Nigel Petherbridge admitted somewhat ruefully. He coughed delicately. "In fact, only one."

"Morgan Mason," Sebastian asserted, sure of himself.

"Excuse me?" Nigel responded.

"Morgan Mason. The Skirt Man. He's the guy you made this for."

Nigel frowned for about five seconds. Then his face cleared and he said. "Oh, you mean the recently deceased farmer. Dear me, no. This cream wasn't for him. It was for . . ." He shook his head. "I am sorry, Sebastian. But I'm not permitted to tell you for whom I made it. The new confidentiality requirements. Lawsuits and all that. But here. Let me write down the name of the public-health nurse who managed the case."

"Public-health nurse?" Billy said. "I thought only doctors could write prescriptions."

"True. But nurses can pick them up and administer them."

On a small pad and in very neat letters, Nigel wrote: HARRIET KNEELAND.

He added a telephone number and an address.

"Harriet has been nursing for almost fifty years and rather reminds one of the schoolteacher whom every student loves to hate." He held the paper out to Sebastian. "I don't believe that I'm going beyond the bounds of confidentiality to tell you that the compound cream about which you are asking was prepared for a woman who was undergoing radiation treatment and who was suffering from a post-traumatic skin disorder."

"A woman?" Sebastian repeated cautiously.

"Oh, yes. In fact, in all the years I've been dispensing drugs, I have never yet been asked to provide it for a man."

chapter 21

SEBASTIAN DID NOT telephone Harriet Kneeland for an appointment. He and Billy just drove to the address Nigel Petherbridge had written down and pulled into the driveway of a small, tidy, angular brick house with bright white shutters and four immaculate brick steps leading to the front door

Billy said, "Remember the pig's house in the fairytale? The one the big bad wolf huffed and puffed at but couldn't blow down?"

"What about it?"

Billy inclined his head toward the door.

"This is it."

Sebastian knocked and waited.

The house was sitting on about a quarter of an acre of well-kept lawn. On either side of the front door were gardens containing healthy azaleas, rhododendrons, junipers, and holly. A brick path leading to the door from the driveway was bordered by rows of hosta. Behind the house, the yard dropped sharply off and became a high bank of the Susquehanna River.

"My vacation is over on Sunday," Billy told Sebastian. "If we pull out Nurse Kneeland's fingernails, what are the chances of us being able to wrap up this case by then?"

Sebastian opened his mouth to answer, but at that very second the door was yanked open, and the imposing figure of Harriet Kneeland appeared.

With unerring instinct, her eyes flew to Sebastian.

"You are the state police investigator," she said. Her eyes shifted to Billy. "You are the sidekick."

"Supervising Fire Marshal Bill Nightingale at your service." Billy inclined his head in a polite bow.

"Nigel Petherbridge called and told me about you. Wipe your feet on the mat and come inside."

She turned and marched into her living room.

Sebastian and Billy looked at each other.

Billy whispered sternly out of the side of his mouth, "You're tracking dirt."

Sebastian grinned.

The two men followed Nurse Kneeland into the formal living room and sat where she directed them on a stiff Victorian sofa. She positioned herself rigidly opposite the sofa on a high-back Queen Anne chair with her hands clasped neatly in her lap.

"State your business," she said, much in the same way that a schoolteacher might command, "Conjugate your verbs."

Harriet Kneeland was a reed-thin woman in her early seventies with a narrow head shaped like a vitamin capsule. She had silver-streaked light brown hair permed into tight curls, perfectly round black eyes, and thin lips firmly pressed together as though they were incubating phrases of disapproval.

"I do not violate patient confidentiality," she said. "However, the patient you are asking about had no family and is dead. Before I tell you anything else, I should like to know the nature of your inquiry."

State police investigators, as a rule, ask the questions. They do not answer them. However, Harriet Kneeland was clearly one of those for whom rules were designed to be broken. So Sebastian told her about the fire and he showed her the jar that had been found in the woods behind the Skirt Man's house.

"Spontaneous human rubbish," she snapped crisply, momentarily resting her flinty black eyes on Billy's face. "I take it that your involvement with this investigation stems from the fire."

"Yes, ma'am," Billy answered obediently.

"What is your opinion of that ridiculous television show?"

Billy risked a grin.

"That it *was* ridiculous."

Nurse Kneeland nodded.

"I am glad to see that you aren't a fool." She unclasped her hands and rested her palms on knobby knees covered by the thin material of her floral-print dress.

"The jar you've shown me appears to contain a cream that was prescribed for a former patient of mine, Allison Downs. As a consequence of the radiation treatments that Mrs. Downs was undergoing, her skin was extremely sensitive and easily irritated. Application twice daily of this compound alleviated her symptoms somewhat. As to why the jar was found in the vicinity of Mr. Mason's house, I have no idea. It had never been prescribed for him."

At first, Sebastian wasn't sure he was hearing Harriet Kneeland correctly. He shot a look at Billy.

"Excuse me," Sebastian said. "But are you saying that Morgan Mason was your patient, too?"

Harriet Kneeland lifted one hand and cupped it firmly over the other.

"That is correct."

"What was Mr. Mason's problem?" Sebastian blurted out. Then, seeing her lips tighten and her eyes harden, he softened the question. "I mean, what was he being treated for? Medically."

"I," she said, her eyes immobile on Sebastian's face, "was not his nurse at the time of his death."

"Before he died, then? What was his—"

"Complaint?" Billy suggested.

Harriet stood up.

"I do not believe it would be appropriate for me to discuss it."

Sebastian also stood.

"Miss Kneeland," he began.

"It's *Mrs.* Kneeland," she said firmly. "My husband is dead."

"So is Morgan Mason," Sebastian persisted. "Nothing that you tell us can hurt him, and it may help us to find his killer."

Harriet smoothed out the wrinkles of her dress. "Nevertheless, I have nothing further to say. However, I have no objection to your contacting the public-health nurse who took over for me after I retired."

"Who?" Sebastian and Billy both said at the same time.

"She is also the Killdeer town historian. Her name is Lillian Roadigger."

Before either man had time to react, Harriet Kneeland turned to Billy.

He thought, but wasn't certain, that he saw the barest glimmer of amusement in her eyes when she added, "Presumably this information will make it unnecessary for you to pull out my fingernails."

chapter 22

SINCE THE *County Courier and Gazette* hits the newsstands on Thursday, I usually make that my no-show day, and I fill up my TO DO list with chores like "Swing on the hammock," "Watch the hollyhocks grow," and "Take Murdock out for a drag."

Murdock is our basset hound.

He has extremely long ears, which he habitually steps on. I have seen him stand in one place for what seems like hours, a stricken look in his eyes as he moves neither forward nor backward, captive to the paw he does not realize is imprisoning his ear.

If I were to open the door of our house in Fawn Creek, beckon Murdock to me, and indicate the intoxicating delights of the surrounding fields and the woods behind the hedgerow, including an abundance of squirrels, chipmunks, and rabbits to chase, he would simply stand in that doorway with a look of betrayal on his face as if to say, "*You* who are supposed to provide for my happiness, *you* who are supposed to

love me, *you* wish to send me out into a wilderness of om-
nipresent threats and certain death?"

Murdock, alas, is a city dog.

He was adopted from a shelter in Manhattan, and when
Merry, then a little bit of a thing herself, took him for his
debut walk, the first thing that his paws touched was con-
crete, the first air that he breathed was fortified with exhaust
fumes, and the first critter he chose *not* to chase was a pizza
deliveryman.

Murdock does not chase things.

He is sublimely uninterested in nature, and his idea of
exercise is to rotate his head from his water dish to his food
dish.

Which is why I was about to drag him for a walk when
the telephone rang. Unfortunately, I got two of Murdock's
legs and one ear entangled in his leash, and I was not able to
reach the telephone until after my nail lady had left a peremptory message on our answering machine.

"Annie, it's Pam. Meet me for lunch at The Coffee Shop at
11:30. I'll have half an hour before my noon appointment.
Bring a pad and a pencil. You're buying."

And she hung up.

The place we were to meet is about two blocks from Nails
by Pamela and has a red neon sign. It is a relic from the
1950s, but fortunately one of the owners, probably fearing
that a customer would disappear through the torn vinyl of
the cushion into the deteriorating foam inside, had recently
reupholstered all of the seats in the booths that lined three of
the shop's four walls.

Other than the jukebox and the coffee, The Coffee Shop
had very little to recommend it. The hamburgers were leathery. The pie tasted like cardboard. And the waitresses all had

that unfortunate look of having had too many children, too few husbands, and too tired feet.

But the booths were comfortable and the coffee was good.

Pam had arrived before me, ordered us two cups of fresh brew, and started talking even before I sat down.

"I never would have believed it of Rose," she said, leaning forward eagerly.

Then she told me what the assistant bank manager, the real estate agent, and the town clerk had told her in the utmost confidence and how she figured out what Rose Gimbel had done.

chapter 23

AFTER MY LUNCH with Pam, I had a feeling that things were coming to a head and that a certain amount of pressure exerted upon Slim Cornfield might be in order to make sure that whatever eruptions ensued would be emanating from the right volcanoes.

So, once again I arrived uninvited at my boss's house. His car was in the driveway and he answered the doorbell after the first ring.

"Oh. It's you," he said and abruptly turned away. Since he hadn't thrown a machete at me, I followed him inside.

The worst thing that you could say about Slim's house was that nothing had a place, and nothing was in its place.

But oh, what things!

Models of single-propeller airplanes dangling by invisible threads from the ceiling; stacks of pre–World War II issues of the *Saturday Evening Post, Life,* and *Look* magazines; a working model of the solar system with planets that revolved around the sun; a fish tank containing exotic fish with orangey pink tails that swirled behind them like scarves of floating chiffon.

On Slim's desk were a white-boned skull with a corncob pipe clenched between its teeth, a miniature locomotive replete with passenger cars that spun around the desk's perimeter on an itty-bitty railroad track, a gyroscope, and an ink bottle flaunting a flamboyant green quill pen.

The dictionary that Slim regularly consulted was one of those four-hundred-pound tomes that our parents used to put under our bottoms when we were too small to reach the dining-room table.

Hanging on the wall behind his desk was a huge limited-edition print of the Constitution of the United States with a beautiful depiction of the founding fathers in a narrow mural running along the top, and the entire two bottom shelves of Slim's bookcase were filled with first editions by Edgar Rice Burroughs, including *Tarzan of the Apes, The Eternal Savage,* and *The Land that Time Forgot.*

The room, like the man, exuded unpredictable elements of irrepressible boyhood. Also like the man, it suggested a potential for chaos—for being neither here nor there.

Slim lifted a stuffed owl off a cushion on the sofa, sat down, leaped back up again, and strode into the kitchen. He jerked the refrigerator door open, took out a carton of orange juice, poured two glasses, and gave one to me. Then he put his glass down on the counter, pushed open the screened kitchen door, and walked outside, where he began to pace back and forth on the small patio.

I followed him.

"Why are you so nervous, Boss?" I asked, trying not to be trampled when he made a sharp right turn.

Not only did he not answer, but I knew something was mightily wrong when he didn't try to blow my head off with his usual "I'm not your boss" retort.

I moved a few inches closer.

"What happened when you met Rose Gimbel?"

Slim stopped, spun around, and stared down at me. The look in his eyes was so intense that I was instantly immobilized. I felt as though he had grabbed me by the throat.

"Rose is . . . Rose is . . ."

I stared right back at him. Waiting.

Then he closed his eyes, shook his head, and literally crumpled into the patio chair behind him. I pulled over a similar chair.

"I take it the two of you met?"

Slim nodded.

"Did you go to her house?"

He nodded again.

"You drove to her house. Did you call her first?"

He shook his head.

"Okay. We're making progress. You got out of your car and rang the doorbell. Then what?"

Slim hunched over in his chair and tilted his head up at me. I swear he looked like Quasimodo.

"She . . . She . . ."

I put my hand to my ear. "Sounds like? Two-syllable word?" I gave Slim an exaggerated scowl. "Did she ask you if you were a Jehovah's Witness? Did she sic the dog on you? Did she hit you over the head?"

Come to think of it, Slim did look as if he had been hit over the head.

"She . . . She . . ." I continued to mock him. "She *what*, for heaven's sake?"

Slim then gave me a confounded look that was so downright appealing, I could have hugged him right then and there. His next words underlined the look.

"She's *nice*," he said.

What could I do but smile?

Rose Gimbel *was* nice.

A clichéd word that perfectly captured the essence of her soul.

"Why are you so surprised?" I asked Slim.

He unfolded his body a fraction, and his voice was barely audible. "I thought that I was interviewing a criminal."

I raised an eyebrow. "That remains to be seen, doesn't it? When you asked Rose about her connection to Hobby Hills, what did she tell you?"

A mulish look settled into the angular planes of Slim's boyish face.

"I didn't ask her."

I pretended to be shocked.

"You didn't ask Rose what you went there to ask her about?" My voice was laminated with sarcasm. "What *did* you talk about?"

The resolve fled Slim's face as quickly as it had come, and he slumped back against his patio chair. Then in the quietest and most gently musing of voices, Slim Cornfield told me what he had learned about Rose.

How throughout her childhood she had expected great things from her grownup self—to become a wartime photojournalist, to work in a laboratory and discover a cure for Alzheimer's, to become a test pilot, or to invent an economically feasible energy source.

How her parents' health started to fail before she went to college, and she gave up her scholarship at Penn State to attend the state university at Binghamton, so she could commute back and forth to Killdeer and take care of them.

How instead of majoring in journalism, she enrolled in library science.

How instead of setting her job sights on the *Daily News*

or the *New York Times,* she was hired by the Four County Library system and assigned to the bookmobile.

How she bought a little house up the block from her parents, and did what she had to do until the day they died.

"Did she ever tell you about 'the eventual Rose'?" Slim asked, a wistful smile on his much-too-vulnerable face.

That was a new one to me.

"No. Tell me."

"The way she explained it," Slim said, "there are two Roses. The Rose who lives alone in her little house, reads adventure novels, takes care of her flowers, mows her lawn, and goes to work every day."

He paused for a moment.

"Go on," I urged.

"And then there is 'the eventual Rose,'" Slim went on. "She going to fall in love someday with the right man, be happy, make him happy, work at a job she loves, have children, and find a way not to regret the life of adventure that she didn't lead."

He took a shallow breath that expelled into a deep sigh.

I studied my boss.

It was plainly visible that Slim was wearing his heart on his sleeve. I also saw a curious hesitancy on his face and in his eyes that hadn't been there the day he had consigned his appointment calendar, belt, and watch to the wastebasket.

"The eventual Rose," I said, "sounds exactly like the eventual Slim. Except that Rose's glass is filled with lemonade and yours is filled with lemons."

He looked at me oddly.

"You know," he said. "You're right."

"Of course I'm right." I leaned forward and slapped my knees. "Now. About my story."

Slim frowned. "What story?"

"The one about Rose Gimbel, the Skirt Man, and Hobby Hills."

Slim looked puzzled. "There is no story! I never talked to her about Hobby Hills or—"

I cut him off.

"Not a problem," I said with ruthless good cheer. "Turns out I got everything I need from a different source. I can see the headline now. ROSE GIMBEL MISAPPROPRIATES TAX-PAYER DOLLARS FOR . . ."

Slim shot to his feet.

"I won't have it!"

I also stood up.

"*You* can't stop it!"

Then, carefully arranging what I hoped was a look of smug superiority on my face, I added in a cooler tone of voice, "Not, at least, as long as *I* am editor in chief!"

chapter 24

A COMBINATION of circumstances had recently altered the futures of both Killdeer and Hobby Hills. Predominant among them was the shutting down of two major industries in town within the same twelve-month period.

The first to do so was the Royce-Barton typewriter factory. You may not remember Royce-Barton by name but I would be willing to bet that you would recognize one of their venerable old machines if you saw it in an antique store or museum. Boxy yet somehow beautiful with its glossy black enamel casing, gleaming chrome carriage return, and brass-trimmed keys.

Since the factory opened in 1886, Royce-Barton had kept up with constantly evolving technology and had successfully introduced portable typewriters, electric typewriters, and even word-processing machines. Computers, however, tore a big hole in the last pontoon that had been keeping the company afloat, and sadly, the doors to Royce-Barton were padlocked forever.

Redfield Plastics, the other factory to close, had moved to Killdeer in 1906. For more than a century it had manufactured plastics, paints, and glues, eventually expanding to the other side of the river and employing over two hundred people. But those days were long gone, and six months after Royce-Barton went to the big manufacturing conglomerate in the sky, Redfield Plastics joined it.

Other than the loss of jobs in the area, the most excruciating problem these plant closures created was the loss of tax revenues. Thousands upon thousands of dollars that the village and town of Killdeer had counted on to pay salaries and maintain roads, parks, schools, and the library had suddenly disappeared.

Problems of this nature, of course, were not limited to Killdeer. Villages, towns, and cities all over the world have struggled with empty coffers from the day the first hunter-gatherer stopped sneaking around the bushes and said to his brethren, "Let's build a road."

Since then, they have all implemented the same tried, true, and despised solution.

Taxes.

When Rose Gimbel accepted the job of tax assessor for the village of Killdeer, she had expected it to entail a certain amount of clerical work, a certain amount of tabulation and calculation, and some—but not much—reassessment. Most of that, she was told, would arise from the sale or purchase of property that had not been assessed in many years.

Rose Gimbel had been the tax assessor for less than eighteen months when Killdeer's two major manufacturing companies ceased to exist. Their departure generated her first crises as a village employee and forced her to be what she later called "an institutional bad guy."

Being "bad," she suddenly realized, was the largest part

of her job description. Indeed, it was what she had been hired to do.

Rose was charged by law with the responsibility of reassessing all of the homes, businesses, and properties in Killdeer. According to a predetermined formula, she would have to raise everybody's taxes by 50 percent.

Poor Rose.

Never had a civil employee or petty bureaucrat been so ill-equipped to play the heavy.

Never had a tax collector been so keenly aware of the condition and plight of her potential victims.

Rose took an inventory of her options.

There were nine hundred and ninety-seven people living in the town of Killdeer. Over five hundred of them lived in the village proper.

She pulled up the tax rolls on her computer and began to scroll through the names.

Lydia and Frank McCutcheon, 27 Faircrest Road. Their son, Richard, had been Rose's music teacher in seventh and eight grades. His car had stalled at a railroad crossing and he had been instantly killed by an oncoming train. Lydia and Frank had been dairy farmers until they retired, sold their farm, and bought that nice little two-bedroom house in town. The house was paid for, but other than their Social Security checks, the old people had no income.

They could not afford a 50 percent tax increase.

Carmen Lockerly, 13 Hill Street. Carmen was old. She was one of the very first Girl Scouts in New York and she had helped found the Ladies Auxiliary of the Killdeer Volunteer Fire Department. She and her husband, Lester, had owned and operated the Lockerly Bakery from 1942 until his death in 1987. After she sold the bakery, Carmen took up quilting and, despite her failing eyesight, continued to donate ornate bedspreads to the Killdeer Museum for their raffle at the annual arts and crafts show.

She could not afford the tax increase.

Chester Josephson, 14 Main Street. Chester had inherited the barbershop and the small house next door from his father, Ansel. Both were sour men. Until his death, Ansel gave the worst haircuts in the county. Now Chester did. The farmers liked to go to him because it annoyed their wives. It's not that Chester actually ruined the looks of anybody who sat in his barber chair, but nobody ever came out of there improved.

Chester was unmarried, and three years earlier, his brother, Preston, prematurely afflicted by the early stages of Alzheimer's, had come to live with him. Preston swept up the barbershop, made coffee (usually forgetting to add coffee grounds), and occasionally wandered off only to be brought back by good-hearted high school kids.

Even with the disability check that Preston brought in, money was never flush at 14 Main Street, and if Rose raised Chester's taxes, he was either going to have to learn how to give good haircuts or he would have to sell his house.

Rose continued to scroll down the names.

The Browns, the Underwoods, the Wickhams, the Voorhees.

So many neighbors. So many longtime residents who had spent their lives in Killdeer. What was going to happen to them?

Rose shut down her computer and pressed her fingers firmly against her forehead. The inside of her skull felt like a runway for jumbo jets.

She dropped her head to her desk.

The words "What am I going to do?" swirled around in her head as they dodged the incoming planes.

chapter 25

SONNY AND MOE'S platform when they ran for mayor was that Killdeer had more problems than whether or not Victorian cupolas should be added to Federal houses or owners of private property should be tarred and feathered if they put plastic squirrels on their front lawns.

Hobby Hills, they explained, was the biggest problem.

Hobby Hills was a blister on the foot of Killdeer. It was a canker sore on the upper lip of the town.

To pull back a single fold on the curtain concealing future events, it might be prudent now to tell you that, although Sonny and Moses Dillenbeck were smart, funny, inquisitive, loyal, resourceful, and tenacious, they were not particularly conversant with New York State election law, and when they decided to replace Morgan Mason as candidates for mayor, their lack of familiarity with legal formalities would have interesting repercussions down the road.

Six days after the Skirt Man's death, though, neither the Dillenbeck boys nor anyone else in Killdeer cared a stitch about what Sonny and Moe could *not* do. We were focused only on what we thought they *could* do.

Sonny and Moe's overall goal that Friday night was to crash the party at Hobby Hills, while at the same time remembering that if my beautiful, brown-eyed daughter came back with so much as a mosquito bite, her father and I would kill them. Their specific objective was to meld in with the crowd, evaluate the operation, and look for something they could take out with them that would give the state police a reason to arrest Domingo Nogales Ramirez or to shut down Hobby Hills.

"As the future mayors of Killdeer," Sonny and Moe announced in a speech they were practicing in our kitchen, "we will do everything within our power to eliminate the sale and distribution of illegal drugs to our local youth."

That they were our local youth seemed to have escaped their attention.

"Get off your soapbox and sit down," Sebastian ordered.

Although in the course of his duties with the state police my husband is often compassionate, as a father he is ruthless.

They sat.

Meredith walked in.

At this point, I would normally have said that Merry floated, drifted, waltzed, glided, or wafted in. Despite what I had often considered to be Merry's ineradicable "ballerina-ness," however, she had managed to eliminate from her person any and all indications that she might be anything other than an ordinary, sloppy teenager.

Merry's bright red hair was tangled into two disheveled braids, and the khaki brim of a battered fisherman's hat hid half her face. She was wearing a black Grateful Dead tank top with ragged hip-hugging blue jeans that revealed a diamond-studded belly-button ring. There were cheap plastic flip-flops on her feet.

I would like to be able to maintain my membership in the worthy-to-be-a-mother club by claiming that her appearance caused my heart to palpitate and my palms to sweat, but in fact, I had helped to dress her.

Pam, who not only did my nails but also administered my covert information retrieval system, had been appointed our unofficial wardrobe mistress for the day. Merry's belly-button ring—clipped on and removable, thank God—had come from Pam's jewelry box. The tank top and blue jeans had come from the back of her closet.

Merry stood before us in the kitchen.

Forgetting herself for the moment, she straightened her back and pirouetted gracefully.

Sonny leaped to his feet, grabbed each of her shoulders, and crunched them together.

"Slouch," he ordered.

She slouched.

"Now turn."

She turned.

"Not like a dancer," Moe said.

"Like a loser," Sonny added.

Merry extended one bare foot; her toenails, I suddenly realized, had been painted chartreuse. Before she had completed even one-quarter of a revolution, she tripped and barely avoided falling down, or so it seemed.

By the time she had regained her balance, there was about her the boneless slovenliness that one usually associates with the lost souls, vagrants, and bums who scrounge cigarette butts from the gutter, wrap themselves in old blankets, and live on the streets.

Good heavens, I suddenly realized. All of those pantomime lessons we had paid for at the McKenzie School of Ballet were actually paying off!

Moe Dillenbeck clenched the air with both fists and let out a loud "Woo hoo!"

Sonny nodded appreciatively. "Undeniably unsavory."

Billy, always Merry's most loyal fan, leaned back in his chair and began to applaud.

I joined in.

"Darling," I said. "You look positively pestilent."

Sebastian, who could hardly stand to see a scrape on Merry's knee let alone the complete submergence of her personality into this creature of despair, grunted, "I hate it. I don't want you to go."

Merry began to laugh. It was such a pretty sound. Like Edgar Alan Poe's tintinnabulation of the bells, bells, bells, bells, bells.

She stood, walked over to her father, got up on her tiptoes, and kissed him on the cheek.

"Don't worry, Daddy. I won't get hurt."

Sonny Dillenbeck nodded.

"Not a scratch, sir."

Moe stood up and crossed to his brother. "We'll protect your daughter."

Billy also stood. He moved toward Sebastian.

It was really quite cute.

Sonny and Moe, shoulder to shoulder opposite Sebastian and Billy, also shoulder to shoulder, with Merry looking quite the disreputable elf at the center of all that testosterone.

"You had better," Billy said.

Moe saluted.

Sonny clicked his heels.

Livingston ate the pompons off my slippers.

———

BY THE TIME the kids were ready to leave, even my husband and brother had to admit that all three teenagers had become indistinguishable from the usual flotsam and jetsam that congregated by the Quick-It Mart and hitchhiked, walked, or drifted toward Hobby Hills.

Sonny, who on his way out of the womb had made up his mind to be an actor, had allowed a few days' growth of blond bristle to sprout on his handsome jaw. There wasn't much he could do with his short hair, so he dyed it blue. When he saw me staring at him in disbelief, he said, "It's vegetable dye, Mrs. Merry's mom. It will wash out."

The gray sleeveless sweatshirt he was wearing exposed muscular arms on which were tattooed—impermanently, he assured me—a heart with a serpent wrapped around it and a casket bearing a ghastly death's head.

The biggest surprise was how he had so effectively transformed all visible aspects of a boy named Sonny who had a disposition that was, well, sunny into an angry, bitter, hostile, and belligerent youth whom people would walk around the block to avoid.

Moe, whose soul dresses up every day in a fireman's turnout gear, had decided upon a less-is-more approach. He had perched a pair of wire-rimmed eyeglasses on his nose, bunched his curly hair into a stubby ponytail, threw on a yellow-and-purple tie-dyed T-shirt, and said, "I'm the class nerd. Merry and my brother are going to corrupt me."

"What do you three expect to achieve with this masquerade?" Sebastian asked, still unconvinced.

Sonny and Moe, their answers rapidly interweaving, said, "We want to know how they deal drugs inside Hobby Hills and—"

"—if alcohol is sold to minors. Scratch that. We know it's sold to minors. We want to prove that it is."

"We'll nose around to see if there's any talk about Mr. Mason."

"If anyone saw something the night he was killed."

"If anyone *did* anything."

"We'll do some nonspecific, all-purpose snooping."

"Case the joint."

"Play it by ear," they ended together, pulling their tongues into parking spots at exactly the same time.

Sebastian turned to Merry.

"And you?" He was trying to sound stern and paternal. "What's your justification for this irrational escapade?"

Merry took a deep breath and smiled with her eyes and her heart. She sighed blissfully.

"Tonight is my senior prom, Daddy."

I laughed.

The "I was dancing so hard I never had a childhood" theme was once again rearing its mischievous head.

Sebastian stared at our daughter for a few exasperated seconds. He grunted. "Some prom." Then he said, "Okay, you three. Fashion show is over. Sit down. Billy has something to say to you."

Billy stood up. He rested his knuckles on the kitchen table and leaned forward.

"Before we let you babes wander into the freak-infested woods, we are going to bring you up to date on every aspect of this case. The saying 'What you don't know can't hurt you' is dangerous. What you don't know *can* hurt you. Particularly during an undercover operation."

Billy moved away from the table.

"Origin-and-cause investigation. Autopsy results. Interviews. Evidence. You're going to hear it all and you're going to hear it now." He reminded me of a squadron leader briefing his pilots before a particularly perilous bombing run. "We'll start with the fire at the Skirt Man's house."

And that's exactly what he did.

He went all the way back to Morgan Mason's body. Where it had been. How it had looked when he and Sebastian had arrived on the scene. What was left of it. And what the burn patterns meant.

He explained that the tobacco pipe they found had been tucked into the cushion of the Skirt Man's chair to mislead them.

He read excerpts from the autopsy reports, and detailed how bodies burn, why they cannot burn spontaneously, and why the fire in the living room hadn't extended beyond the limits of the chair that was the origin of the fire.

Then he moved aside and let Sebastian take over.

Sebastian summarized their interview with Domingo Nogales Ramirez.

He described the search for a pharmacist who could identify the jar that Sonny and Moe had found behind the Skirt Man's house. He produced the jar, unscrewed the lid, and let them smell the cream inside.

He gave synopses of his interviews with Lewis Firth, Decidia Skirball, Andrew Mason, Neverly Mason, and Harriet Kneeland.

Then he yielded the briefing back to Billy.

Billy described our return visit to Morgan Mason's house, Creedmore Snowdon's videotape, and our discovery of a coin under the radiator in the Skirt Man's foyer.

Sonny, Moe, and Merry sat stone-still at the kitchen table as my brother and my husband talked. Their eyes reflected the work that their brains were doing as they tracked the history of the investigation from physical evidence to interrogation to interview and back to physical evidence again.

The instant Billy stopped talking, the Dillenbeck boys exchanged one of their telepathic glances and said simultaneously, "Can we see it?"

"See what?"

"The coin you found in Mr. Mason's house."

Sebastian reached into his pants pocket. He took out a small plastic evidence bag about the size of a business card.

Inside the bag was the 1922 silver dollar.

Sebastian dumped it into Moe's outstretched palm.

Three youthful heads bent down and studied it together. Sonny plucked it out of Moe's palm and held it up between his thumb and forefinger.

He looked at Moe.

Moe looked at Sonny.

They both nodded.

Then Sonny turned to Sebastian and said, "Our dad sells these."

chapter 26

WHEN I THINK BACK to the night my daughter and the Dillenbeck boys went to Hobby Hills, my brain switches into documentary mode and I see the evening as a rerun of an exposé on teenagers, alcohol, and drugs.

After Sebastian and Billy finished their briefing, they drove the kids to the east side of the Susquehanna River in Killdeer. Nobody saw Merry, Sonny, and Moe get out of the Jeep and nobody saw them slouch toward the Quick-It Mart two blocks away to mingle with the others on their way to Hobby Hills.

A pickup truck driven by a Hell's Angels wannabe, replete with scraggly beard and bandana, became their means of transportation to the alleged music festival and they arrived at their destination a few minutes before 9:00 P.M.

They bought their tickets at the gate. On each ticket were printed the names of the bands that were going to provide the entertainment. From 10:00 to 11:00 P.M.: *Fractured Wrists.* From 11:00 P.M. to midnight: *Paid Assassins.* From midnight to 1:00 A.M.: *Mono Nukes.* From 1:00 to 2:00 A.M.: *Rat Poison.*

Until the first set began, recorded music filled the air, doing its part to inflict irreversible damage to the attendees' eardrums.

Everybody looked awful, according to Merry. She, Sonny, and Moe looked awful, too, and blended in so well that they couldn't make their way to the food counters, bathroom, or bandstand without being accosted by enterprising individuals trying to sell them Ecstasy, LSD, marijuana, peyote, or cocaine.

Sonny said he was approached by a man wearing eye shadow and a peasant blouse who seemed to want to buy *him*. And so many deviant-looking Homo sapiens came up to Merry with offers and suggestions ranging from—well, never mind. Suffice it to say that if Merry had wanted to be mortified with embarrassment, she could have. If she had wanted to overdose and die, she could have done that, too.

Our trio wandered from clusters of high school dropouts and leftover hippies to lone losers zoned out on music, memories, and mescaline. Sonny never left Merry's side and acted as if he were so stoned or drunk that he couldn't stand upright without her support, but he was really holding on to her so that nobody else could get close.

Moe would periodically amble off alone to strike up conversations with the bartender, the disk jockey, the guy who sold tickets at the gate, or the anorexic woman smoking Marlboros outside the food court. She was the one who told Moe that she had overheard Domingo Ramirez muttering, "If that stuttering asshole comes on my property one more time, he's a dead man," after the receding figure of an old man driving an ancient tractor down the winding driveway at Hobby Hills.

Then she asked Moe out on a date.

What they saw and heard confirmed every terrible thing we had suspected about Hobby Hills.

Drugs were dealt freely and illegally.

Most of the teenagers who had come there were on the verge of alcohol poisoning or drug overdoses.

All of the adults there were drug dealers, drug addicts, or worse.

Laws were being broken and children were at risk. Unfortunately, all of those acts were being performed on private property, away from the prying eyes and law enforcement capabilities of the state police.

How to get what was *inside* Hobby Hills *outside*. That was the problem Merry and the Dillenbeck boys had to face.

"What are our options?" they speculated as the night progressed.

And then they saw her.

Sonny dug an elbow into his brother's ribs.

"Sondra!" he whispered urgently.

Merry and Moe followed Sonny's line of vision, and there she was.

Long blond hair framed her heart-shaped face; heavy black liner rimmed her gray-blue eyes, giving her the look of a terrified raccoon. She was wearing bleached jeans and a tight tube top that accentuated her skinny legs and flat chest. A squiggly object that looked like a giant sperm dangled from a gold chain around her neck; beaded bracelets jangled on each of her thin wrists.

Her lipstick was so pale that it was almost white.

She was thin, young, and frail, with the delicate bones of a sparrow.

Her face was perfect.

If she continued with what seemed to be her current lifestyle, she was going to make a beautiful corpse.

"Can't be," Moe objected, peering over the tops of his eyeglasses.

"It's her, all right," Sonny said firmly.

"Jesus!" Moe shook his head the way someone would at a roadside accident. "She's only twelve years old!"

Merry put her arms around both boys' shoulders and pulled their heads toward hers.

"Tell me." Her voice was low but emphatic. "Tell me everything."

And they did.

The girl leaning against the outdoor bar and nervously biting her lower lip was Sondra Brody.

Her father, Clifford Brody, ran the appliance department at Dillenbeck Hardware. His wife had left him eleven months after Sondra was born, moving (rumor had it) to a commune in Oregon and never communicating with them again. Clifford Brody was a single father. Sondra, something of a daddy's girl, was eager to please the proud and protective parent who would clearly do anything for his adored child. Sonny and Moe's mother, Netty, had been something of a surrogate mother to Sondra, often accompanying Cliff to girls' clothing stores to help him buy her the right outfits for such esoteric occasions as her first boy-girl party dress or her first field trip to a museum. Sonny and Moe themselves had also been called upon to keep an eye on Sondra when Cliff's babysitter did a no-show and he had to dash off to an emergency electrical repair.

Nobody ever minded Sondra's presence at Dillenbeck Hardware where she was a rare and happy distraction. Sonny remembered how every Christmas, Netty would dress Sondra up in an elf outfit, give her a basket, and have her hand out candy canes to customers, all of whom instantly fell in love with her innocent friendliness and sweet smile. Moe told Merry about the summer Sondra decided she wanted to be a cowgirl and insisted that he teach her how to ride a horse.

Since Moe had never been on a horse, he borrowed a friend's saddle and he taught her how to ride a fence instead.

Until about a year ago, Sondra had been everybody's favorite little sister, little daughter, and little friend.

Then her mother came back.

First name: Emma. Last name: Cone.

Profession: Attorney.

Licensed to practice in: Oregon, Washington, and New York State.

Last known cause: Defending the privacy rights of terrorists.

Best known for: Representing radical environmentalists who broke into a chicken farm to liberate eggs.

New assignment: Open an office in Norwich, New York, to defend the rights of anyone arrested for the illegal sale, use, promotion, or distribution of nonprescription drugs.

Address: 103 River Road—a one-year rental located half a block from the house where her ex-husband and daughter lived.

"Sondra started to get weird right after her mother came back," Moe told Merry. "First she was a goth. Then a slut. Now she's doing 1960s love child."

"What does her mother look like?"

"Sondra," both boys said at the same time.

"Then she's beautiful?"

"If someone else lived inside her body, maybe she would be beautiful, but not Emma Cone." Moe turned to his brother. "How would you describe her, Sonny?"

"Hard. Flinty. Mean. Fanatical. Mom says she's one of those women who aren't happy unless they can sacrifice everything for a cause."

"Including their own children?"

Sonny and Moe nodded.

Merry studied the child in question. Sondra Brody was

leaning against the bar in a provocative—if you could call anything a twelve-year-old does "provocative"—pose.

"Do you think that her mother is *using* Sondra?" My daughter began, clearly dismayed.

The boys expressed no doubt that she was.

"After Emma Cone moved back to Killdeer, Sondra changed," Moe said.

"She stopped coming into the hardware store."

"She told Cliff she wanted to live with her mother."

"She wouldn't talk to me or Moe anymore."

"She started to play hooky and hang out with losers. Her grades dropped from As and Bs to Ds and Fs. Poor Cliff doesn't know what to do about it. He can't go to his wife's house and drag his daughter back. Dad recommended an attorney, but all the stupid lawyer says is 'These things take time.'"

"Do you think Sondra's mother knows that Sondra is here?" Merry asked.

"Unless her daughter is posing for pictures, holding a poster, or marching in a protest parade, her mother doesn't care where she is. Cliff doesn't know, I can guarantee you that. If he did, he'd probably kill her."

"Sondra?"

"No. Emma."

Just then, Domingo Nogales Ramirez walked into the open area between the bandstand and the food counters, looking confident, menacing, and—unlike ninety-nine percent of the people at Hobby Hills—sober. He strode to the bar and parked himself hip to hip next to Sondra Brody. He lifted his left hand and held up two fingers. The bartender placed two Budweisers in front of him. Domingo popped both cans open, slid one over to the twelve-year-old and winked at her.

Sondra's raccoon eyes opened even wider.

"Oh, my God," Merry said, and she started to move forward.

Sonny and Moe whispered, "Stay."

Domingo Nogales Ramirez lifted his beer can to his mouth and stared down at Sondra. Waiting.

Sondra reached for her own can, obviously terrified.

She touched it to her lips. Her narrow chest was heaving so hard that all Merry could think of was *Run, Bambi. Run.*

Then Ramirez laughed. Not his previous ha-ha laugh. A big, guttural, pig laugh. He cupped his left hand like a man about to squeeze a basketball and grabbed Sondra's small prepubescent ass.

She dropped her beer can.

She dropped her arms.

She stared at Domingo Ramirez.

He put his arm around her shoulders and tried to lead her away from the bar. She didn't budge.

Sonny pushed Merry behind his body and called out, "Sondra!"

Sondra turned.

Moe moved to Sonny's right.

"Come on, cowgirl!" he shouted.

Sondra wretched herself away from Domingo Ramirez and ran straight into Moe Dillenbeck's arms.

They moved quickly.

Merry said she didn't know if they had cleverly used the crowd to evade Domingo Ramirez or if he had simply moved on to another beer and another girl, unconcerned that the twelve-year-old to whom he had just served liquor had suddenly disappeared.

It took our brave trio less than five minutes to reach the Hobby Hills entrance, half-leading, half-dragging, and half-carrying Sondra Brody all the way. They hadn't gone another

fifty feet before, as Merry described it, "Daddy's Jeep materi-
alized out of nowhere."

Sebastian and Billy leaped out of the front seat.

"Are you all right?"

"Yes, Daddy. We're fine."

"Are you sure you're all right?"

"Yes, Uncle Billy. Where did you come from?"

Then *I* got out of the backseat.

"Are you all right, darling?" I asked. Admittedly, we could
have used a dialogue coach. But ask any parent. Fear for one's
offspring rarely inspires Shakespearean prose.

"*Mother!*" Merry exclaimed in that disparaging way
teenagers have of making you feel as if you have three heads.

Sebastian motioned all of us out of the way.

He stood in front of our daughter.

He looked very tall, very stern, and very New York State
Police.

When he planted his fists on his hips, all I could think of
was a displeased genie about to have words with someone
who had rubbed his magic lamp the wrong way.

"Prom's over," he said to our daughter. "Get into the car."

chapter 27

THE KITCHEN OF our house in Fawn Creek became Command Control for the entire Skirt Man investigation. It was from there that the foray into Hobby Hills had been launched and to there that we returned with a shivering Sondra Brody clinging to Moe Dillenbeck like what she was, a terrified child.

As soon as we got home, we wrapped a blanket around Sondra's trembling shoulders, put hot cups of tea in front of her, and called her father. But it took Cliff half an hour to get to us.

During those thirty minutes, not only was Sondra willing to talk, it would have been impossible to prevent her from doing so.

Poor little thing. Even now my heart twists when I think of her.

"My...my...mother..." The words came out in sobs and gulps. "I...I...always wanted her to come back and be...be...be my *mother*."

The sentences didn't flow.

The thoughts weren't particularly coherent.

But there was a gist to it all that was inescapable.

"She...came...came back to...to...I thought she loved me, but..."

Emma Cone had returned to Killdeer, rented a house a few doors away, and set about to cultivate her child.

"She...she...brought me to...to...her office. There were reporters, and she....she...they took lots of pictures."

The articles that subsequently appeared in our local newspapers dealt at length with Emma's new law firm and her old ties to the community—ties dating back to the birth of her daughter. Neither the articles nor the press releases made reference to where Emma had been or what Emma had been doing during the eleven plus years between Sondra's birth and the press conference.

"I...I...always wanted a mother to...to...take me shopping and to...to...kiss me good-night."

Since her reappearance, not once had the woman taken her daughter shopping.

Nor had she asked Sondra to live with her. The child had simply packed up her stuffed animals, toothbrush, and pajamas and moved in.

"I...I...tried to...to...get her to...to...love me."

The outfits—dressing goth, dressing slut, dressing hippy— were all attempts by Sondra to attract her mother's attention. To remake herself from the trusting, adorable, happy-hearted adolescent she had been into something that would keep her mother in Killdeer and make her mother love her.

As the story unfolded, I came to hate Emma Cone. Really hate her. So did Sebastian. So did Billy. So did Merry, Sonny, and Moe.

"What were you doing in Hobby Hills?" I asked Sondra.

Finally the trembling began to subside.

"I wanted to see where my mommy..." Then she suddenly gasped, as if she had caught herself on the verge of an act of betrayal. "I mean my *mother.* She doesn't like me to call her Mommy. She says it makes me sound like a baby. I ... I wanted to see where my *mother* works."

Okay, I said to myself.

One. Emma Cone reunites with her reasonably well-adjusted but desperately vulnerable daughter, whom she had abandoned twelve years before.

Two. She does not want the child to live with her.

Three. She lets Sondra move in so that she can use her for publicity and promotional purposes.

Four. Mother-daughter photographs printed in the newspapers imply that Emma had not opened a law office in Chenango County merely to defend drug dealers, but that she has roots in the community.

Five. Thereby suggesting that she was just another local attorney, plain and simple, practicing law.

"Had she ever taken you to Hobby Hills before?" I asked, wrapping Sondra's icy hands around her hot mug.

"No. But, but we drove past it on ... on the way to her office."

"Drink your tea."

Sondra raised the cup tentatively to her lips. I could see blue veins through the pale skin of her delicate hands.

"Merry," I said. I motioned toward the counter.

Merry nodded. Seconds later she was back with a big platter of cookies and brownies. I don't think that I have ever seen anything quite so tremulously sad as a teardrop falling from the tip of a child's eyelash onto the surface of a chocolate chip cookie.

"He ... he is a bad man," Sondra said, hiccupping back a sob.

I took the cookie out of her hand and placed it down on her plate.

"Who is a bad man, dear?"

"Mr. Ramirez."

"How did you come to be there with him tonight?"

I was asking all the questions. When, if, and until this became an official state police investigation, we were taking no chances that a defense attorney would accuse Sebastian or Billy of entrapment, kidnapping, or anything else that might imply they had somehow illegally crossed a line.

"Mommy . . . I mean Mother didn't come home tonight. I called her and called her, but she never called me back, so I thought she . . . she might be with Mr. Ramirez at . . . at Hobby Hills."

Then she really started to cry.

The only other thing we got out of her that night was that she had tried to look older so that no one would challenge her when she bought her ticket to get into Hobby Hills. Not only had nobody challenged Sondra, they hadn't even asked her age. We also learned that she had taken the $100 admission fee from a stash her father kept in his sock drawer.

That revelation was followed by a recurrence of the trembling and the sobbed admission, "I want my daddy."

Oh, God. What a night.

Clifford Brody finally arrived. He barged into our kitchen with fear, anger, love, and relief raging across his face like a manic slide show.

Sondra threw herself into her father's arms.

More tears.

More hiccups.

chapter 28

DID DOMINGO NOGALES RAMIREZ murder the Skirt Man? Did he set fire to Morgan Mason's body and plant a tobacco pipe in the cushion of his chair to make it look like an accidental fire?

I didn't know.

I did know that whether or not he was a murderer, the temperate climate of Mr. Ramirez's life was about to change.

There was the matter of serving liquor to a minor. A minor who with her father's encouragement would be willing to testify against Ramirez in a court of law.

There was the matter of child molestation and/or child endangerment charges involving the same minor. Same father. Same testimony. Same father's blessings.

There was the matter of the credibility of Ramirez's attorney, since similar child endangerment charges were in the works against Emma Cone who, Sebastian discovered the next day, had packed up her bong, closed her law office, and disappeared.

There was the matter of Domingo Nogales Ramirez's real-estate taxes. Or, as I like to refer to it in my tap-dancing heart, *The Iniquitous Instance of Rose Gimbel and the Diabolical Drug Lord.*

My informant in this matter was Pamela Gilbert, my belly-button pierced nail lady.

Pam's confidential sources—think women with their fingertips soaking in soapy water—were, in the order that she developed them, Gillian Williams, Marilyn Roosevelt, and Bess Bonner.

Let's start with Gillian Williams, who, according to Pam, always wears pale pink nail polish and does not like her cuticles cut.

Gillian was a mere slip of a girl, barely twenty-seven years old, a college graduate with a BA in liberal arts, and no skills whatsoever. She started in the Norwich branch of the Killdeer Savings Bank as an executive trainee. A few years later, she was transferred to Killdeer, where she assumed the responsibilities of assistant vice president. Most of her work involved mortgages and home equity loans.

Gillian had mousy brown hair, eyes and eyebrows that curved into symmetrical half-moons, and a smile that wasn't exactly sad but never quite managed to light up her face. As a rule, she never discussed the bank's clients. But Pam, being a force of nature, was as adept at extracting pertinent facts, unsubstantiated speculations, and irrelevant details from her clients as an oral surgeon is at extracting teeth.

Gillian told Pam that Domingo Nogales Ramirez did not own Hobby Hills outright. He had a mortgage. In effect, he co-owned the former horse farm/music venue/campsite with the Killdeer Savings Bank. Before approaching Gillian Williams several months earlier, he and the bank had each owned about half. After he submitted an application for a second mortgage, the Killdeer Savings Bank owned eighty-five per-cent of Hobby Hills and Ramirez owned only fifteen.

"Did he refinance to get a lower interest rate?" Pam asked, filing the left side of Gillian's right thumbnail.

"No. He just increased his debt to the bank by a hundred thousand dollars."

Pam filed the right side of Gillian's right thumbnail.

"Why?"

"Why does anyone refinance their properties?" Gillian asked rhetorically. "To get more money."

Pam moved on to the left forefinger.

"What was Ramirez's attitude when he came in? I'm betting he was his usual swaggering, belligerent, and egomaniacal self."

"No." Gillian shook her head. "Mr. Ramirez was ... " She frowned, struggling to find the right word. Then her frown disappeared and she finished confidently. "He was *smug*."

MARILYN ROOSEVELT was honest, well-groomed, thirty pounds overweight, and forty-five years old. She wore her ash blond hair in a neat pageboy, had braces on slightly buckteeth, and owned Picket Fence Realty, a small, thriving company in a diminutive white house that had been converted to an office. It was located half a block from Nails by Pamela and its yard, not coincidentally, was bordered by a picket fence.

Marilyn was convivial, friendly, enterprising, and aggressive. She was the president of the local Rotary Club, and she loved to talk.

"And then," her mouth was already in gear as she entered Nails by Pamela, "he throws the door to my office open, and he's standing in the entryway looking nasty enough to chew hubcaps."

"Sit," Pam commanded.

Marilyn deposited her not insignificant posterior in a chair opposite my nail lady. She thrust a hand forward.

"Of course, I recognized him right away, because the *Courier* prints his picture every time someone new drowns over at Death Lake. He glared at me for a few seconds before he said anything. He's scary, Pam. Then he moved toward my desk and . . ." Marilyn pulled a small bottle out of her purse. "What do you think about this? It's called Lemon-Tangerine. It's a perky color, don't you think?"

Pam gave the bottle a disdainful glance, opened Marilyn's purse, and dropped it back inside. "It's revolting. Stick with Plum Mist."

"I always do Plum Mist. I'm tired of Plum Mist. I hate Plum Mist."

Pam jerked a bottle off the shelf and held it out.

"Fancy Nancy?"

Marilyn unscrewed the top of the nail polish, pulled out the small brush, and studied it for about five seconds. She gave it back to Pam.

"Okay. Fancy Nancy."

Pam undid the latch on Marilyn's watch, removed three rings, and plunged the Realtor's hand into a bowl of warm water.

"So. What did he do?"

"He stomped over to my desk and growled, 'I want to sell my property'. I asked him who he was and where the property is, even though I knew perfectly well. I gave him applications to fill out, and we were getting along famously—like a rabbit in a cage with a rattlesnake, and let me tell you, *I* wasn't the rattlesnake—when, next thing you know, we come to the line on the form for the asking price and . . . ouch!" Marilyn wrenched back her hand. "You just gouged a hole in my finger!"

Pam pulled the hand back. "Don't be such a baby. How much did he want?"

Marilyn leaned forward.

"You're not going to believe this."

Pam leaned forward.

"Try me."

"All right. Mr. Ramirez, the notorious owner of the Hobby Hills Horse Farm. Mr. Ramirez, manager of a campsite where, over the years, more than—"

"Marilyn," Pam said impatiently. "I've got a customer waiting. Cut to the chase."

The real estate agent smiled. Sun glinted off the braces binding her teeth, and she announced, triumphantly, "He wants *three million dollars!*"

THE CUSTOMER WHO had been waiting her turn at Nails by Pamela was Rose Gimbel. Rose had also been present, her nose buried in a magazine, when the assistant vice president of the Killdeer Savings Bank disclosed the refinancing particulars of Domingo Ramirez and Hobby Hills.

Being the tax assessor for the village of Killdeer, Rose was more aware than most of the dire consequences awaiting the town as a result of Royce-Barton and Redfield Plastics going out of business. She was also in a perpetual state of panic at the prospect of causing her neighbors to lose their homes.

Rose cogitated on the knowledge she had acquired during her two years as tax assessor.

She cogitated on the information that she had acquired while waiting for her turn with Pam.

Rose had always known that a drastically increased sales price on a property that had originally been purchased for much less could be a reason for a tax reassessment. She now also knew that Domingo Ramirez considered Hobby Hills to be worth millions of dollars more than he had previously admitted.

Rose went over the variables in her mind:

- Killdeer had lost approximately $75,000 in tax revenues when the two factories had shut down.
- $75,000 in taxes would somehow have to be raised to prevent the village from going bankrupt.
- Hobby Hills was paying real-estate taxes based upon an assessed value of only three hundred thousand dollars. This was two million seven hundred thousand dollars *less* than the price Domingo Ramirez was asking for his property.
- Rose did a quick calculation in her head, disregarding tax guidelines, protocols, charts, and comparative properties, and she arrived at a new tax figure of . . . what a coincidence!
- $75,000.

Rose smiled.

Killdeer's deficit would be met.

The anticipated problems of the McCutcheons, the Lockerbys, the Josephsons, and the Browns would not materialize. Rose would not have to raise *their* taxes.

She would raise the taxes on Hobby Hills.

Domingo Ramirez, no doubt, would sue the village. He had done so in the past. This time he would claim discriminatory taxation, if there were such a thing. In response the village board would subpoena the application he had filled out for Marilyn Roosevelt at Picket Fence Realty.

Ramirez's own handwriting would testify against him.

Rose spent most of that night at her computer in the village offices.

In the whispery quiet hours of the morning, she went home tired but happy.

And when her head touched the pillow, she slept the sleep of an avenging angel, supremely confident that justice would be done.

chapter 29

THERE WERE, if you recall, *three* women whose nails Pamela had manicured and from whom she had extracted vital bits of information. I have already told you about Gillian Williams and Marilyn Roosevelt. I have not yet told you about Bess Bonner. Bess was the Killdeer village clerk. On Friday and Saturday nights, she also waited tables at the Maple Leaf Restaurant, which happens to be one of our favorite eating places in Fawn Creek.

My knowledge of Bess, although essentially superficial, was at least comprehensive enough to recognize her excellent memory (she never got an order wrong), her inquiring mind, and her commitment to vicarious living. Although I was quite sure the main reason Bess worked a second job was to make extra money, I was equally certain that she had chosen the Maple Leaf Restaurant because she liked people.

When I say "people," I am not referring to the often-disgruntled citizens who popped into the village offices on a daily basis to demand that their roads be repaired, their neighbors' dogs be impounded, or the four boys who comprised the entire population of Killdeer's skateboarders be banned from the village streets.

I mean regular people. People without problems. People with an appetite for life who were out for an evening of good food, pleasant company, and uncomplicated fun.

When our daughter was growing up, Sebastian and I used to take Merry with us to the Maple Leaf about once a week. If Billy was in town, he would come along as well. In those early days, we merely exchanged pleasantries with Bess as she took our orders and served our food. However, time passed, a casual friendship evolved, and it became one of my great delights to watch her trying to pry stories out of "Fire Marshal Bill."

She loved hearing him talk about investigations, burn patterns, and bad guys being caught. That same fascination applied to Merry after she had become a professional dancer and joined the Delacourt Ballet Theater. When Bess wasn't bringing us glasses of water, baskets of rolls, and bowls of pumpkin soup, she would urge our daughter to tell her about everything from the colors, styles, and textures of her costumes to what Merry was feeling while she waited in the wings before going on stage.

I surmised that Bess's having a husband who sold sporting goods and two sons for whom the sun rose and set on the condition of their high school football uniforms meant that her emotional cup did not exactly floweth over; in her heart of hearts, she longed, if not for danger and adventure, for at least a bit more in terms of conversation.

Being of a practical bent, she got it from her favorite customers at the restaurant.

Occasionally, something of sufficient interest to bear repeating would happen during the course of her work as the Killdeer village clerk. When it did, Bess Bonner's psychic metronome would begin to tick.

The events surrounding Rose Gimbel and her tax assessment not only caused Bess's metronome to tick, they pushed the tempo of her emotional life into high gear.

From the minute she had flipped that first Maple Leaf Restaurant menu down on top of our plates, the whole family liked Bess Bonner. She was one of those pleasant women who have always looked and will always look middle-aged. She had naturally rosy cheeks, wispy hair the color of ripe peaches, and cheerful triangular eyes. She had only been going to Nails by Pamela for six months when I developed an urgent need to know why Rose Gimbel was no longer functioning as the Killdeer tax assessor. Given Pam's mystical ability to make tongues wag, coupled with Bess's natural inclination to wag her tongue, there was no question that we had found our source.

"Good grief," Pam said, grabbing Bess's right hand. "What have you been doing with this? Stringing barbed wire?"

Bess looked ruefully at her chapped hands and jagged fingernails.

"I've been helping out in the kitchen at the Maple Leaf. The guy who washes dishes called in sick."

Pam shook her head. "Next time wear gloves." ·

Bess sighed deeply. "Let's hope there is no next time."

Pam gently balanced Bess's fingers on the palm of her hand. "Your nails are a mess. How about a new set? Men like long nails. It'll drive your husband crazy."

Bess studied her hands.

"I've never had fake nails before."

"Well, it's time. I use silk. It's more expensive than acrylic, but it looks more natural."

"How long does it take?"

"An hour, give or take. I don't have any appointments

until after lunch and your hands really are a fright. What do you say?"

Bess Bonner said, "Yes."

During that hour and a half, Pamela got the entire story.

MEETINGS OF THE Killdeer Village Board always take place at 7:30 P.M. on the second Wednesday of each month. They are held in the back office of the town hall where an American flag stands in a corner between two battered oak desks. Framed pictures of children, dogs, and grandchildren grace the surfaces of the desks; three shelves hang on brackets behind the desks. To the right of the shelves are a series of file cabinets. On top of the middle file cabinet are a rotating fan, a stack of pamphlets, a philodendron, and a rack of ink stamps labeled PAID, PAST DUE, SECOND NOTICE, URGENT and RECEIPT ENCLOSED.

On the critical night in question, half of the chairs in the room had been placed around a large metal table at which the members of the board gathered to tend to the business of the village. The rest of the chairs were arranged in three short rows for any townspeople who chose to observe or participate in the meeting.

The Pledge of Allegiance was recited.

The meeting was called to order.

The village clerk read aloud the minutes of the last board meeting. Then she took attendance and turned the proceedings over to Roy Milligan, the village supervisor, who owned a dairy farm over on Loose Plank Road.

The meetings of the village board were open to everybody, and a lot of everybodies came to make requests or vent their spleens. On a typical night, village officials might have to deal with problems ranging from negotiations with cable television companies to a VFW request for money to purchase markers for veterans' graves.

Dealing with village business generally took anywhere from one to two hours, depending upon the number and complexity of the items on the agenda. It was only *after* the open meeting had wound down that a motion was made to go into executive session, which is not open to the public.

During executive session, questions of a sensitive nature are dealt with. Questions such as Rose's reassessment of the taxes on Hobby Hills.

"Rose, I'm not sure I can come up with the right word to describe the recklessness of the course of action you have undertaken," the village supervisor said.

Bess Bonner, who secretly admired what Rose had done, lifted a pencil to attract the village supervisor's attention.

"Daring?" she suggested.

Roy Milligan's shoulders slumped forward wearily.

"Yes, Bess. It was daring. But the word I was groping for is 'dangerous.'"

He turned to Rose and observed her silently. He continued to do so until she looked in his direction.

"I am afraid, Rose, that playing Robin Hood with our friend Ramirez was like tying a firecracker to a tiger's tail. We now have a very angry tiger at our door."

Rose said nothing. She simply seemed sad. Her posture—head held high on her swanlike neck—betrayed no evidence of defeat, and her dark auburn hair was wound into its characteristically tidy French twist. Only her chic little spit curls, one over each ear, seemed to be unraveling dispiritedly.

"As you know, Mr. Ramirez has sued us yet again. This makes..." Roy Milligan turned to the village clerk. "How many lawsuits has he got against us now, Bess?"

"Six."

"Including this one?"

"That's right."

He drummed his fingers against the tabletop and stared speculatively at Rose.

"Our dilemma is that we, as a board, cannot appear to be behind this preposterous scheme of yours." His voice hushed to a whisper and he leaned forward confidentially. "Even though we all agree that it was a brilliant plan."

Rose's eyes widened in surprise and her lips quavered at the edge of a smile.

The village supervisor did not return her smile.

But it was clear to everyone in the room that his sun-drenched eyes were twinkling and his farmer's heart was glad.

"SO, THEN WHAT happened?" Pam asked, sufficiently absorbed in the story that she had unwittingly given Bess's nails a third coat of polish.

"Then the village supervisor asked Rose to hand in her resignation. He said that Seth Christopher, Fawn Creek's tax assessor, would assume Rose's responsibilities. He also said that the new tax assessment on Hobby Hills would remain in place."

Pam's mouth literally dropped open.

Bess basked silently in the manicurist's response.

After a few seconds, Pam recovered sufficiently to say, "What else?"

"Nothing else. Roy told us that we shouldn't discuss what had happened outside of executive session; he swore Rose to secrecy, made her promise that she wouldn't tell anybody what she had done, and we all went home."

Pam shook her head.

"I don't believe it."

"Gospel truth."

Then my nail lady folded her arms across her chest, leaned against the back of her chair, and smiled an Eighteenth-Avenue-Brooklyn smile.

"So that son of a bitch lost a round to our little Rose."

Meanwhile, the village clerk looked down at her nails. They were long, gently rounded and had been painted fire engine red.

"I like them!" she exclaimed happily.

Pam made a fist with her right hand and feigned a gentle punch at the village clerk's shoulder.

"And I like *you!*"

chapter 30

THE MORNING AFTER Merry's excursion into Hobby Hills, Livingston disappeared.

Thumbtacked to his stall in the barn was this note. The penmanship, I thought, was pretty good for a goat.

To Meredith Bly

Dear Miss Bly,

Although I have enjoyed my stay in your friendly abode, it is time for me to return to my secret life as a goat. There are many reasons why I must do this. The foremost one is that your ardent admirers only work part-time, and their father makes them put most of their money into a college savings account. Therefore, they could not afford to buy me outright.

I am but a borrowed goat.

At 11:00 o'clock Saturday morning, I must be returned. Despite the mutual desires on the parts of my benefactors to bring happiness to the heart of their future wife, they figured out that when you are on tour, a great ballerina might have other preferences for a roommate than a creature such as myself.

Therefore, it is with great sorrow that I bid you adieu, knowing that if we do not meet again in this world, we will be joined for all eternity in the next.
                    Your loving friend,
                    Livingston

The wisdom of goats!

For, as Livingston no doubt surmised, all good things, even wonderful ones such as our darling daughter's summer vacation, must end. Billy, too, had to be back at his base by nine o'clock on Monday morning to recommit himself to the burn patterns and fire-setters of New York City.

But Monday was still two days away, and Saturday was un-folding before us with its own assortment of responsibilities.

Merry's were the most enviable. After reading her goat note, she contributed a wink, a laugh, and a very tiny tear to Livingston's departure and then retreated with a book to our hammock under the trees.

I set out in our Jeep to find my former boss, Slim Cornfield.

And Sebastian and Billy headed to Dillenbeck Hardware to talk to a man about a silver dollar. The man in question was Boyd Dillenbeck, father to Sonny and Moe, and also, much to my and my husband's surprise, a dealer in collect-able coins.

Sebastian and I had been to Dillenbeck Hardware on dozens of occasions over the years. That is where we bought our washer, dryer, microwave oven, refrigerator, stove, bird-seed, wood chips, light bulbs, and mops.

However, it had never dawned on either of us to scoot past the counter where keys were copied and locks were sold and visit the glass counter where rare and old coins were on display.

"I wasn't much interested in them myself," Boyd Dillenbeck explained as he led Sebastian and Billy to this remote corner of the store. "My father started to collect coins when he was a fireman. After we opened the hardware store, he bought and sold them here as a hobby. When he died, I kept the counter open more out of respect for him than anything else. But damned if I didn't get into it myself. Now, I'm as much a collector as I am a dealer."

Boyd Dillenbeck is an interesting man. The son of a fireman and the father of a prospective fireman, he seemed to be nothing more than a regular guy living a regular life in a regular town. If you had asked him why he hadn't followed in his father's footsteps to become a fireman himself, he probably would have just shrugged and replied, "It wasn't in the cards."

Although Boyd's biological son was Moe, the only physical attribute they had in common was their race. Both were black. Moe, with his gangly body, big hands, big ears, and galooty face, didn't look like anybody in particular, and he particularly didn't look like his father. Sonny, in spite of his fair skin and blond hair, in some funny ways *did*. Both were slim. Both were of medium height. Both had fine bones and strong jaws. And both were extremely handsome.

Boyd was well known in the community for his generosity and his good business sense.

Because he had sent his sons to Gladys Pinch's house to get her wedding ring out of the kitchen sink, they had been rescued by the Skirt Man on Route 39.

Because he had borrowed from the bank to add equipment rental and machine repair to his hardware store, people came from miles around to shop there, and then remained to patronize the other merchants as well.

Because of his good business sense and foresight, a strong trickle-down effect had reenergized the entire town.

Boyd Dillenbeck stood behind the glass counter at the back of his store and watched as Sebastian opened the little plastic bag. The hardware store owner held out his hand, and then placed the coin on a small rectangular pad that was sitting on the countertop.

Boyd took out a magnifying glass and began to study the coin. First one side. Then the other.

"This is a 1922 silver dollar," he said. "It was minted from 1921 to 1935 and was designed by Anthony de Francisci to commemorate the end of World War I." He reached under the counter, pulled out an old-fashioned ledger, and started to thumb through the pages. After searching for three or four minutes, he dropped his hand to a line midway down a page. "My father sold it sixteen years ago, not long after we opened the store. The date of sale was December 18. Let's see what else Dad wrote."

He leaned closer to the ledger.

"It contains .77344 ounces of pure silver and is .900 fine." Once again, he examined the coin through the magnifying glass. "There is a large die break on the neck of Miss Liberty that continues into the word 'Trust,' and there is another die break across her hair that continues into the word 'Liberty.'"

Boyd placed the magnifying glass back on the counter, closed the ledger, looked up, and smiled.

"My father sold it for $45.00."

Sebastian and Billy did not smile back.

"Who bought it?" Billy asked.

"Oh," Boyd Dillenbeck remarked casually. "You want to know that, too?" But he winked when he said it, because he had known all along that obtaining the name of the purchaser was the reason that Sebastian and Billy had come into the store.

"A very fine lady indeed," he chuckled happily at his little joke. "Every year Lillian Roadigger buys another silver dollar." He looked fondly at the coin. "This was her first."

He lifted the ledger off the countertop and was about to restore it to the display case when Sebastian shook his head and held out his hand. Boyd Dillenbeck hesitated for a moment. Then he relinquished the account book, returned the silver dollar to its little plastic pouch, and handed that back to Sebastian, too.

SEBASTIAN AND BILLY did not say a word to each other as they strode down the aisle to the front of the store.

They did not utter a single syllable as they pushed open the front door and continued outside.

They were equally silent, each absorbed in his own bleak ruminations, when they proceeded across the street and walked past Sonny and Moe. The boys were standing in front of the town hall, five feet away from Sebastian's car, listening intently to Bess Bonner.

None of the three noticed my husband or my brother as they walked by.

"I don't like it any more than you do." Bess's voice was authoritative, sympathetic, and loud. "When Creedmore Snowdon came to my office yesterday, I wanted to give him a good thump on the head. He didn't say so, but I think he's afraid that if he runs against you boys for mayor, he'll lose. He's right. He *would* lose! But he's right about the election law, too." She patted Sonny and Moe consolingly on their shoulders. "I wish I could ignore the New York State Constitution, but section three of the Public Officers Law states that anyone running for mayor has to be at least eighteen years old. And, as Mr. Snowdon so emphatically pointed out, on the day of the election, you two boys will still be only seventeen."

chapter 31

I GUESS I SHOULD have called him first, but the probability of finding Slim Cornfield in his garage and having him hurl more gardening tools at me must have appealed to some subconscious hankering I have to live life on the edge. Instead of warning Slim that I was coming, I just barged in.

Or tried to.

He wasn't home.

I checked the turnaround behind the house for his car. It wasn't there.

I started to wonder if he hadn't followed through on his threat to leave town altogether, so I peeked in his living-room window. His model airplanes, fish tank, and pipe-smoking skull were still all snugly in place.

Hmmm. I thought for a minute. Where could Slim be?

I drove to Rose Gimbel's house. Don't ask me why. Wishful thinking, I guess.

I did pretty much the same thing at Rose's that I had done at Slim's. Her car, too, was nowhere to be found, and in her living room, everything was placidly where it had always been.

Which left only one more place to look. So I got back into my car, and I drove to the offices of the *County Courier and Gazette*.

Yes, indeedy.

They were there.

Slim and Rose had parked their cars two spots away from the space I pulled into, right in front of the entry to the *Gazette*. Since the building is always closed on Saturdays, I used my key to get inside. I tiptoed like a thief through the reception area, turned left at the water cooler, and came to a silent standstill outside my office door.

But was it still my office?

I crept forward.

"And that's what she said." Slim's voice could barely contain his fury. "That as long as she was editor in chief, she could publish anything she wanted to. And she's threatening to write all about it. You, the tax reassessment, Domingo Ramirez, and Hobby Hills."

Rose raised her gentle voice in protest. "I know Annie Bly very well, Slim, and I know she would never do that."

Slam!

My former boss's hand crashed into the table.

"Damn right she won't. Not as long as *I'm* the *Courier's* editor in chief."

"But you aren't," Rose interjected reasonably. "Yesterday when you introduced yourself, you told me that you had—"

"Retired? Well, I'm unretiring. This is *my* office. This is *my* desk. This is *my* newspaper. And Annie Bly works for *me*. There are things I want to do and changes I want to make here that have nothing to do with her."

Slim paused. He added in a calmer voice, "You are one of them, Rose."

Nobody said anything for a few long seconds. I stopped breathing.

Rose asked tentatively, "What do you mean?"

"I want you to write for me, Rose. You're a librarian. Write about what you've read. Which books you like. What's going on at the library. Events. Acquisitions. Sales. I see it as a weekly column. Do you think you would be interested?"

"I . . . I . . ." Rose began. There was a sweet breathlessness in her inability to respond.

"Of course, it would mean that we would have to see quite a lot of each other." Slim's voice kept getting softer and lower.

I took one soundless step away from the door, my ears still attuned to my boss's crooning exposition of ideas and Rose's falteringly affirmative responses.

As I continued to back away, I sent a silent benediction toward the occupants of that room.

I could go back to sleeping late, missing deadlines, ignoring breaking stories, and being a short-brained freelance reporter.

The gods had smiled upon me.

I could be irresponsible again.

I was no longer editor in chief!

chapter 32

I WAS DRIVING SOUTH on Route 7 on my way back from the *County Courier and Gazette* when I saw Sebastian's car parked in front of The Coffee Shop in Killdeer. I screeched to a halt, pulled into a space, and was sitting in a booth opposite my husband and my brother less than a minute later.

Sebastian was staring down glumly at his knuckles. Billy was glowering at Boyd Dillenbeck's ledger of coin transactions as though it had just leaped up and slapped him in the face. They told me what they had learned at Dillenbeck Hardware.

No wonder they were so depressed.

"What about a motive?" I asked, my psyche scrabbling through the murk of incriminating evidence for a lapse, a contradiction—anything that would point us away from a woman whom I had wanted to think of as a friend.

Billy shook his head.

"Establishing motive isn't necessary when you're building a case of arson. All you need is an ignition source, a combustible, and an opportunity. For the ignition source, the fire could have been started with a match. The chair and the Skirt Man were the combustibles. And I hate to say it, Annie, but if your nurse friend really was assigned to his case, she had opportunity in spades. She knew him and she had a reason to be there. All she had to do was knock on his door and hit him over the head with a crowbar."

I made a dismissive gesture with my hand. "Hit him over the head? I don't buy it. Tell me where Morgan Mason *was* when Lillian hit him over the head."

Billy began to enumerate on his fingers. "One. He could have been on the porch. Two. He could have been in the hall. Three. He could have been in the doorway." Billy looked up. "Want more?"

I scoffed.

"Tell me *how* she did it then, Mr. Smarty Pants."

Amazing, isn't it, how quickly a mature woman like myself can revert to being a bullying older sister.

I persisted. "What magical words could Lillian have spoken to make a grown man submit to his own death? 'Bend down here for a second, Mr. Skirt Man, so that I can take a swipe at your brains with this nice little bat.'"

"It wasn't a bat. It was a crowbar."

"And after she hit him, what did she do then? Drag him to the chair? How big was he, Sebastian?"

I turned to my husband who, although unresponsive so far, was not being argumentative at least.

Sebastian did one of those husband shrug things.

Billy answered instead.

"At the time of his death, Morgan Mason was five feet ten inches tall. He weighed one hundred and ninety pounds."

"Humph!" I retorted. "So you think that Lillian Roadigger, who is twelve inches tall and weighs twenty-two pounds, is going to drag a man as big as Morgan Mason was?"

And so it went.

I exaggerated.

Billy was able to provide a reasonable response to each of my objections.

Yes. The jar of lotion found in the woods behind the Skirt Man's house indicated that Lillian Roadigger had been there.

Yes. She somehow could have induced her patient to sit in his chair, and she could have hit him with the crowbar when he was unsuspiciously in place.

Yes. A great knowledge of fire forensics was not required to hold a match or a butane lighter under the very dry and highly ignitable upholstery of the seat.

Yes. Since flammable liquids were not introduced, Lillian could have fled from the house without incurring a risk of flashover damage to herself.

Yes. There was enough oxygen in the room to turn the chair into a funeral pyre and sustain combustion long enough to burn Morgan Mason's body, causing his skull to explode.

Yes. Yes. And yes.

"But *why?*" I pleaded, angry, frustrated, and stymied by my own uncertainty. "Why, Billy? People don't kill each other for no reason. Nice people don't kill other nice people unless—"

Billy held up a hand to silence me.

"I know, Annie. I know." His voice was soothing. "But the facts contradict your instincts, and, in fact, nice people sometimes *do* kill each other. Even nice people like your friend." He slid out of the booth and stood up. "That is, if she's even the one who did the dirty deed."

I slid out of the booth after him, turned to my husband, and angrily demanded, "Billy's dancing around the subject. What's he talking about? What does he mean?"

Sebastian got up heavily, threw a tired arm over my shoulder, and, for no reason at all, he bent down and kissed me tenderly on the forehead. Then, his eyes still sad, he said, "Billy means that we aren't finished yet."

chapter 33

MY HUSBAND AND my brother did not invite me to accompany them when they questioned Lillian Roadigger. Those who work for the New York State Police Bureau of Criminal Investigation and the New York City Division of Fire Investigation do not encourage wives and sisters to tag along when a prime suspect is being interviewed.

I, however, was also a friend of Lillian Roadigger. A friend who impulsively decided to drop in and say hello on that sunny Saturday afternoon.

Sebastian and Billy, after dealing with such impulses on a day-to-day basis over many years, wisely offered no resistance.

They pulled into Lillian Roadigger's driveway several minutes ahead of me. When I finally arrived, I thought that I saw a flutter of movement to the left of the garage, but I ignored it, cut the engine, and sat for a while, trying to decide upon a method of approach. Should I brazenly waltz up and ring the bell? Should I test the knob to see if the door had been left unlocked? Should I walk in unannounced and shout out a greeting at the top of my lungs?

I was still pondering my options when I heard the soft slam of a screen door off in the distance. I lifted my head and saw Lillian Roadigger leading Sebastian and Billy out of the back of the house to a redwood table in the yard. I remained where I was for another five minutes. Then I quietly closed the car door behind me, walked up the gentle slope separating the driveway from the backyard, pulled out a chair, and sat down, too.

I did not say hello. They did not say hello. For a fraction of a second, Lillian's eyes darted in my direction, but I couldn't read the expression on her face. Fear? Anxiety? Resentment? Grief? Or relief that she had been caught and that the excruciating dread of discovery was finally over.

Billy dominated what seemed to be more of a conversation than an interrogation. As I listened, I recalled how often he had said that cops should never do fire investigations because the only interrogation methodology they know is "bad guy, good guy," and Billy was of the opinion that no arsonist would confess unless you approached him with a "good guy, better guy" technique.

Billy wasn't just good. He was the best.

Without seeming to be doing so, his vividly blue, non-judgmental eyes took stock of the woman sitting across from him. His voice was relaxed. His whole aspect was respectful. He was an officer of the law. But he was also a defender of womankind. An amiable acquaintance. A country gentleman. A friend.

Oh, Billy.

Dangerous. Dangerous Billy.

The white jar of lotion that Sonny and Moe had found in the Skirt Man's woods was on the table in front of Lillian.

Billy reached out and nudged it forward, but she shook

her head. As always, Lillian was exquisitely groomed. Every short blond curl was perfectly positioned. A pair of tiny diamond earrings sparkled on her diminutive ears. A pair of large, luminous tears glistened in her eyes.

"I don't have to look at it, Mr. Nightingale. I freely admit that it is mine."

Sebastian discreetly flipped through a few pages of notes.

"According to our information, Lillian, this cream or lotion was prescribed for—"

"Yes, I know. It was prescribed for Allison Downs. Harriet Kneeland was her nurse at the time. After Harriet retired, Mrs. Downs was assigned to me. Nigel Petherbridge filled the prescription and I picked it up." Lillian laid a light finger on the lid of the jar. "But I never had the opportunity to meet Mrs. Downs, and I never delivered the lotion. The day before my first visit to her house, she died."

Billy made a tent of his fingers, rested his chin on them for a second or two, and gazed up at the sky. When he looked back at Lillian, his voice was ever so careful. "Which explains why the jar was in your possession, but it doesn't tell us how it got in the woods behind Morgan Mason's house."

Lillian closed her eyes. The two tears that had been lingering there since the start of the conversation began a slow and tortuous descent down her cheeks.

"This jar got inside his house because I brought it there." The matter-of-fact tone in her voice was a disturbing contrast to the tragic look on her face. "I was of the opinion that a compound consisting of camphor and menthol crystals would alleviate Morgan Mason's pain. I have no idea why it was found in the woods outside his house."

Billy leaned forward confidentially. His eyes were compassionate. His voice was low and intimate.

I leaned forward, too, so as not to miss a word.

"What, exactly," Billy said, "was Morgan Mason's diagnosis?"

For almost a minute, Lillian did not respond. She sat upright, like a mannequin bent at a right angle. Then she raised her hands to her eyes, and with her two middle fingers, she wiped away at her tears. It was an admirable effort, but doomed. The tears did not stop. They didn't even slow down.

"In the summer of 1950," Lillian began, her voice expressionless, "Morgan Mason was drafted into the United States Army. Five months later, he was in Korea. A year after that, he was back in Killdeer. He told me that nobody knew he had been drafted, nobody was aware he'd been gone, and nobody welcomed him home. He had fought for his country in what is rightfully called the Forgotten War, and the aftereffects of that year in Korea dominated every aspect of the rest of his life."

Sebastian made one of those throat-clearing noises meant to attract attention.

When Lillian turned to him, he said, almost apologetically, "The Skirt . . . I mean, Mr. Mason stuttered so bad, it must have been very difficult for him to communicate to you what you've just told us."

Lillian frowned. There was a baffled look in her eyes.

"Morgan didn't stutter," she said.

Sebastian didn't say a word.

Billy didn't say a word.

Lillian turned to me.

I said softly, "It took him two weeks to get out a single sentence, Lillian."

But the public-health nurse shook her head. More tears

cascaded out of her eyes, each another shiny diamond of grief. "He never stuttered when he was talking to me."

Sebastian pushed a handkerchief across the table. She picked it up, dabbed at her face, and continued speaking.

"He was wounded in 1951, evacuated to Osaka Hospital, treated, and sent to a rehabilitation facility in Nara, Japan. I'll skip the details of the rest of his time in the army because you only want to know what was wrong with him."

Billy—ah, this was the genius of Billy—said, "Mrs. Roadigger—Lillian—we want to hear anything that you want to tell us."

And so we listened.

After days of evasion, prohibitions, privacy restrictions, and runarounds, somebody was finally going to reveal to us the one thing about Morgan Mason that he had never wanted anyone to know.

The condition Morgan Mason was suffering from, Lillian Roadigger told us, was called post-traumatic reflex sympathetic dystrophy. RSD for short. As well as I can understand it, RSD is a disorder of the autonomic nervous system— don't ask me what that is—which is made up of the sympathetic and the parasympathetic nervous systems.

The sympathetic nervous system controls the blood vessels and nerves that go to the skin. After someone has experienced an injury, even a relatively minor trauma can cut off the blood supply to the skin and set off symptoms.

However, Morgan Mason's traumas had never been relatively minor, and only by keeping any and all irritants away from affected areas was he able to function.

"It was excruciating for him to feel cloth against certain parts of his body," Lillian said; she skimmed a light finger along the lid of the jar. "Cottons. Silks. Synthetics. He couldn't tolerate any of them. But this compound soothed the irritation, reduced the inflammation, and brought him some measure of relief." A huge tear dangled from one of her eyelashes like a Christmas ornament.

It broke away and splashed onto the table.

I looked at Billy. Stunned.

For a few seconds, he seemed to be studying the splat where the tear had landed. Then he raised his bottomless blue eyes to Lillian Roadigger.

"Is that why he wore a skirt?" he asked, softly.

Lillian didn't answer. Instead, for a long, reverent moment, she bowed her head.

chapter 34

WE TOOK A BREAK.

Lillian went into the house to wash her face and reapply her makeup.

I went into the Roadiggers' antiseptic kitchen to root around for a pitcher, a tray, and four glasses. I filled the pitcher with ice water and brought everything outside.

Tough day.

Tough session.

And we weren't done yet.

About ten minutes after going inside, Lillian returned, looking no less sad but considerably more composed. She folded her hands on the top of the table and turned to Billy.

"What else do you want to know?"

Without a second's hesitation, Billy said, "Where were you on the night that Morgan Mason died?"

Lillian turned to Sebastian.

"It wasn't I who discovered Morgan's body," she said guardedly. "It was Creedmore Snowdon. Did you ask him what was *he* doing there? Did you ask him why *he* went to

Morgan's house? Did you ask him what *he* wanted? He was always pestering Morgan. Why wouldn't he leave the poor man alone?"

Lillian was not crying anymore.

She turned to Billy.

"Do I need an alibi? Is that why you're here?"

Instead of answering, my brother pressed on, his voice still gentle.

"What was your relationship with Morgan Mason, Lillian?"

She closed her eyes.

"He was my patient. I was his nurse."

A sparkling tiara of tears formed around her eyelashes, but this time they did not fall. When she reopened her eyes, the remarkable transformation I had noticed the night of the town hall benefit seemed to be making a shadowy comeback. Here, again, was Lillian Roadigger, the butterfly.

But the butterfly's wings were broken and it would never fly again.

"Morgan came into the county health-care system eight months ago with a severe case of pneumonia," Lillian said. "Dr. Chapman, who attended him, asked Morgan questions that nobody had ever bothered to ask him before, and after curing his pneumonia, he prescribed a course of home visits by public-health nurses to evaluate and alleviate Morgan's pain."

"Pain from . . ." Sebastian looked down again to consult his pad.

Lillian cut him off. "Post-traumatic reflex sympathetic dystrophy. RSD. Morgan did not want nurses coming into his house. He did not want anyone, particularly a woman, to violate his privacy. But Doctor Chapman kept after him to try different pain protocols and therapies, and he wouldn't let up until Morgan finally agreed. My first visit was on Monday, January 3."

"You remember the date?"

Lillian smiled. A slight, sad, broken-winged smile.

She tilted her head gently to one side and looked into my eyes.

"I don't know why they say that old people can't fall in love. Do you?" But she did not wait for an answer, because she wasn't talking to me, Sebastian, Billy, or to anyone else. She was speaking to a life that she would never lead. To a missed opportunity. To a ghost on a tractor.

Then she started all over again from the beginning.

"The day I met Morgan Mason, I was fifty-seven years old. It took us less than five minutes to fall in love." She frowned and turned to Billy. "How old was Morgan? I forgot."

Billy turned to Sebastian.

"He was seventy-three years old," my husband told her.

Lillian shook her head perplexedly.

"Think of it!" she said. "To have lived all those years alone in that house, his only friend a dog, his only pleasure reading Western novels, and his body never free of pain."

A soft tilt of her head in the other direction.

A distant, chimerical smile.

"I came into Morgan's life with a jar of someone else's medicine, and for six months, I made an unhappy man happy." The shadow of a smile trembled on her lips. Then the smile disappeared, her voice hardened, and she said abruptly, "But Morgan is dead now, so none of that matters."

She looked directly at Billy. When she spoke again, it was without warmth or recognition. "What else do you want to know?"

For one of the first times in his life, Billy was speechless.

I had neither the will nor the wherewithal to utter a word.

But Sebastian's didn't waver. He reached into his pocket, fiddled for a second with the little plastic bag, and dropped the 1922 silver dollar on the table. It rolled toward Lillian and stopped a few inches from her hand.

She picked it up and looked inquiringly at Sebastian.

"You bought that eighteen years ago from Dillenbeck Hardware."

Lillian nodded.

"We found it after the fire, under the radiator in the entryway to Morgan Mason's house."

The coin fell out of Lillian's fingers.

All of the color drained out of her face. For longer than a minute, Lillian Roadigger was a living, breathing dead woman.

Then we heard a rustle of movement coming from the garage.

I turned and saw Vernon Roadigger leaning heavily on his cane.

He stood motionless. Lillian, too, had heard the sound. Her head jerked toward the garage. Color rushed back into her cheeks and her mouth twisted into a feral snarl.

She leaped up and before anyone could stop her, she was running across the lawn.

By the time Sebastian and Billy caught up with her, Lillian's fingers were wrapped around her husband's neck, and she was banging his head against the side of the garage. Her voice was a jagged gash of pain.

"Why did you do it, Vernon? Why? Why? Why?"

Sebastian and Billy pulled her off.

They had to.

Vernon Roadigger was old and arthritic.

He lay on the ground where his wife had left him slumped like a bag of rot. He had a bitter face and mottled skin.

What I had thought was a cane lay on the grass beside him. It had the same gently rounded handrest as a cane, but instead of ending in a cap, the handle ended in a claw.

It was not a cane.

It was a crowbar.

Vernon did not try to get up. He did not move any part of his body except for his head. He raised it slowly and smoothly.

It was a slithery, snakelike movement.

He sought out his wife's eyes.

Then the son of a bitch smiled.

chapter 35

Memo to file:

Vernon Roadigger waived his right to an attorney and agreed to answer a list of questions submitted to him by the New York State Police. In attendance at the time were Sebastian Bly of the Bureau of Criminal Investigation, Fire Marshal William Nightingale on loan from the New York City Division of Fire Investigation, court reporter Tiffany Bamberger, and technician Jarrod Lyme, who videotaped Mr. Roadigger's responses. During the period of time when we were recording, Mr. Roadigger often digressed from the main thrust of his statement. However, it was agreed upon beforehand that he would be allowed to talk for as long as he wanted to on whatever subject he chose. Although they are not recorded in this transcript, Investigator Bly and Fire Marshal Nightingale interrupted the narrative on several occasions to ask a question or request clarification of a previous answer. Mr. Roadigger appeared to be in full possession of his faculties, and was coherent at the time. A signed copy of his statement is attached:

My name is Vernon Roadigger. I live at 1346 State Highway 204 in Killdeer. I am sixty-eight years old. I retired three years ago as vice president of sales for Medico International. I have two children, ages twenty-one and twenty-three. My wife, Lillian, is a nurse working for the Chenango County Department of Public Health. She is also the town historian. She is fifty-seven years old. Everything that happened is her fault. Her disrespect of me and the sanctity of our marriage precipitated the chain of events that led to Morgan Mason's death. I did not kill him. I was just present at the time that he died.

ALTHOUGH I HAD always liked Lillian Roadigger, she was never what I would call chatty, and her confidences to us came with such painstaking deliberation that I felt they were being embroidered on a satin cushion with a fragile silk thread.

Everything about the relationship between Lillian and the Skirt Man had that same delicate, hand-stitched quality. Even now, when I try to visualize an act of intimacy between the two of them, I do not imagine a crashing together of love-starved bodies, but rather the ever-so-light touch of her still youthful fingers against the leathery palm of his hand.

Lillian slowly and meticulously embroidered a tale that revealed a life of moderate professional gratification, complete emotional deprivation, and profound solitude.

"I have always felt as if I were a bell," Lillian said to me. "A bell that the bell maker had forgotten to teach how to ring.

Year after year I sat in my church tower, feeling the summer heat, the winter cold, and the achingly beautiful breezes of spring. Year after year I waited for the bell maker to come back and teach me how to ring. But he never came back. So there I remained, a bell without a voice, surrounded by a silence so great that I thought I had disappeared."

My wife went to Morgan Mason's house for the first time on Monday, January 3, seven months and twenty-three days ago. I am an orderly man, so I keep track of these things. She had been a good wife until then. Not flitting all over the place like other women. She wasn't gregarious. She wasn't foolish. Lillian knew that her place was at home with the children and me. At least, she did until January 3. After that, she changed. She was like a person possessed. First, she took on that job as the town historian. Job! She didn't even get paid. Then she turned the sunroom into what she called an office. But it wasn't an office at all. it was a rat's nest. Old magazines, newspapers, torn posters. Junk. All over the place. She knows that I am an orderly man. She knows that clutter offends me. She didn't listen to me. She patted me on the head as if I were a dog—I do not like domesticated animals—and she laughed. She said, "A little dust never hurt anybody, Vernon," knowing that I hate dust. Then she began to sing.

Lillian Roadigger continued to be parsimonious with the details of her relationship with the Skirt Man, but from the bits and pieces that she volunteered, I learned a few things. Most of them you already know.

The one that warrants repeating is that when they were together, the Skirt Man *read* to Lillian.

Out loud.

Without tripping over each word.

I am not big on miracles and I do not claim to know anything about loaves and fishes or burning bushes. But I do believe in the miracle of love. Love at first sight. Love at second sight. Love at foresight. Love at hindsight. Love can make cripples walk, drunkards pour gin down the sink, lotharios throw away their little black books, and cowards catch bullets in their teeth.

Love is the most effective balm, therapy, medicine, and elixir in the world.

It can even transform a public-health nurse into a butterfly and teach a shy, stuttering farmer how to speak.

Other than converting the sunroom into what she called an office, Lillian continued to maintain my house in the orderly manner that I require. The rooms were clean; all of my magazines were stacked by date and category in the hall cupboard, kept for three months, and then discarded. Meals were served on time. But she began to experiment with recipes. Enchiladas. Egg drop soup. Hummus. Goulash. Terrible stuff. Not the good, American cooking I like. Tuna noodle casseroles. Fried chicken. Pork chops. Hamburgers. Her mind was all over the place. Buying clothes from catalogues. Chatting on the telephone about the town hall. Lillian never chatted before. She had only used the phone to make appointments or order prescriptions. And flowers. I am allergic to flowers. I can work all day in my vegetable garden, but flowers make me sneeze. She

brought lilies into the house, arranged them in a
vase, and put them in the living room. I made her
throw them out. A husband has obligations to his
family. I fulfill my obligations. I pay the bills.
I take care of the house, my garden, my lawn equipment, and the cars. I have always maintained an orderly existence. I do not philander. I do not raise
my voice. I am reliable and predictable. Lillian is
no longer reliable or predictable. She uses garish
colors on her nails. She giggles. She laughs. She
sings. As I said, January 3 is when the trouble
began. The situation did not become intolerable
until June 17. That was when I began to follow her.

I asked Lillian what the Skirt Man had read to her.

"Poetry."

"What kind of poetry?"

"Cowboy poems. Farm poems. Poems by Will Carleton,
Badger Clark, Stephen Vincent Benét, James Whitcomb
Riley."

At first I thought it odd that the two loneliest men I have
ever encountered—Slim Cornfield and Morgan Mason—
were both enamored of rhyme. Then I remembered how, in
my solitary youth, I had sometimes stood at the window of
my tiny apartment on East Twenty-seventh Street, looking
out the window at the Empire State Building with a cigarette
in my hand for companionship, and I wondered if perhaps
poetry isn't a lonely man's cigarette.

"Was there any particular poem that he liked?" I asked
Lillian.

"No. But I remember two lines from a Badger Clark
poem he used to recite. 'Make me as big and open as the
plains. As honest as the horse between my knees.'"

Lillian added, "Change it to 'as honest as the *tractor* between his knees' and you would have an accurate portrait of Morgan."

```
I stayed far back on the road. Lillian didn't know
that I was following her. I never slowed down after
she turned into his driveway. I never stopped. Ex-
cept for that one time. Seven days ago. On July 16.
I knew that she would be gone all day for the show
at the high school. Everyone in town would be
there. Except for him and me. I didn't go to his
house intending to cause him harm. Not really. I
was just thinking one thing. That I want my life
back the way it was. I don't want flowers in my liv-
ing room. I don't want Chinese food or tacos or egg
drop soup. I don't want my sunroom cluttered with
junk. I don't want my wife raising money to build
a town hall auditorium. I don't want her patting me
on the head like a dog, changing her hairdo, or
painting her nails like a tart. I am an orderly man
who wants nothing but an orderly existence. Is that
too much to ask?
```

One of the things I wondered about from the day I met Sonny and Moe was how those two comedians had managed to ingratiate themselves into the Skirt Man's life. His farmer ethic would have required him to pull their car out of the mud. I understood that. But why had that intensely private and congenitally shy man continued to welcome them into his house, playing chess with them and allowing them access to the intimate details of his conflicts with Creedmore Snowdon, Lewis Furth, Domingo Nogales Ramirez, Decidia Skirball, and his nephew, Andy?

That was a mystery to me.

If I had checked my calendar, I would have figured it out.

Lillian Roadigger met the Skirt Man on Monday, January 3. Five days later, Sonny and Moe Dillenbeck skidded off the road not far from his house.

Obviously, the Skirt Man had started to change on the day that he met the public-health nurse.

"I encouraged Morgan to invite the boys back. To make them feel welcome. To become their friend," Lillian said. "I told him that talking to people was part of his physical therapy and that increased social contact was one of the pain-reduction protocols Dr. Chapman had prescribed."

"Was it?"

Lillian smiled. What a waste that this charming woman had not lived a life of a thousand smiles.

"Not if you asked Dr. Chapman. But it worked. When Morgan was engaged in conversation with those two lovable scamps, he never thought about his pain."

No. I did not bring it along as a weapon. I have used it for years as a cane. I have arthritis. I am not a tall man. It is just the right height for me when I want a little extra support. And it has heft when I'm out in the fields and I need to get rid of a rabbit or a wild dog. I parked my car opposite the satellite dish. I crossed the road and walked through the woods at the edge of his property. A dog started barking. It's just as well that I had my cane. I soon put a stop to that. The dog made the night go bad. That was the beginning. It was an unusual night. A disconcerting night. I did not have a plan. I approached the door directly. I am not a sneak. If I had planned anything at all, it would have been to confront him face to face. Man

to man. See here, I would have said. Your relationship with my wife has disrupted my orderly existence, and it must stop. But that isn't the way it
worked out. The barking dog must have gotten his
attention, because he opened the door before I
knocked. I was not prepared for how tall he was.
How broad. He had thick shoulders. A thick neck. My
first impression was that he wasn't a man at all,
but a tree trunk. He looked down at me without fear.
He had no idea who I was. He said, "Wh...wh...who
are you?" But I was angry. Angry that this defective giant who couldn't even form a sentence had
stolen my wife—had ruined my life. Did I tell you
that I am in the habit of carrying around a silver
dollar? My wife gives me one every year for Christmas. When I am agitated, I sometimes roll it around
in my fingers to calm myself. When he opened the
door, I was leaning on my cane with my right hand
and playing with my silver dollar with my left. It
wasn't fair that I was so small and he was so big.
So I dropped my coin. Instinctively, he bent down
to pick it up. Then he wasn't big anymore. No. No.
I can't account for the hair and blood on the crowbar. Crowbar! I've already told you that it's not a
crowbar. It's a cane. A cane! Yes. Yes, of course,
I remember the jar. It did not belong to Morgan
Mason. It belonged to a former patient of my wife's.
Lillian had no right to give it to anyone else. It
had no business being in that house. Fire? Why do
you keep harping on about a fire? No. I did not drag
his body to the sofa. And why do you call it a sofa?
It wasn't a sofa. It was a chair. Yes. I had a pipe
with me. No. I wasn't smoking it at the time. I
don't know how it got into the chair. Hot? Yes. It
was hot. Too hot. I had to get out of there. No. I

did not set a fire. Why are you tormenting me with
all these questions? I merely went to his house to
discuss an untenable situation. I am an orderly
man. I had the right to protect the orderliness of
my life. Surely, nobody could object to that.

Of course, the partial print on the bottom of the jar was
a perfect match to Vernon Roadigger's thumb. The remnants
of the tobacco pipe found in Morgan Mason's chair were too
far gone for identification, but Billy, who never misses anything, remarked on the pipe rack in the Roadiggers' kitchen
that was missing one pipe. As to the crowbar, there were microscopic particles of blood and hair on the claw. Inside Vernon's garage, Sebastian and Billy found a pair of boots with
dirt on them that matched the dirt in the Skirt Man's backyard. That's where they also found bits and pieces of Buddy's
blood and fur on the cuffs of an old pair of trousers that Vernon had tossed in an old oil drum.

Funny how this scrupulously thorough and pathologi-
cally neat little man had not bothered to clean up these few
pieces of evidence that incriminated him. Funny how he
hadn't bothered to sweep away the tire tracks that, a week
later, were still behind the bushes across from the satellite
dish. Funny, that is, unless for some bizarre reason Vernon
was actually proud of what he had done.

I never can remember the differences between first-degree
murder, second-degree murder, and manslaughter, so I'm
not sure what kind of charges are going to be brought against
him. But I am sure that there is more than enough evidence
for the district attorney to build a compelling case against
Vernon Roadigger, and that Vernon will spend the rest of his
miserable life in jail.

Does that offer Lillian some measure of comfort or relief?

I doubt it.

I think she would rather have killed Vernon herself when she was bashing his head into the side of the garage.

I don't really know, though.

There are many more things that I don't know about the Skirt Man and the public-health nurse who had come to alleviate his pain.

I don't know if they had ever kissed each other.

I don't know if he held her hand when he read to her.

I don't know if he had ever rubbed her feet, or if Lillian had ever buried her nose in the Skirt Man's hair and inhaled the musky masculinity of the man she loved, as I so often do with my darling Sebastian.

I did ask Lillian once if she and Morgan had ever discussed the future—her divorce, their living together, the two of them getting married.

"No, Annie," she replied softly. "We never talked about the future. Why would we? We thought we had all the time in the world."

And as I looked into her solemn, sad eyes, I could not help but think of a bell that had found and then lost its voice again and of a beautiful butterfly with an irreparably broken wing.

chapter 36

LIFE IN KILLDEER continued to percolate even after the discovery of the Skirt Man's killer. We had the excitement of Slim Cornfield, newly reinstated as editor in chief, implementing his own policy on local hard news by giving Vernon Roadigger's arrest a banner headline in the *County Courier and Gazette.*

And despite my threat to report everything about Rose Gimbel's innovative tax reassessments, I did nothing. I had never intended to. I was just trying to scare Slim into going back to his old job and pursuing Rose on a personal level. But I did do a big story on what happened to the former horse farm after our drug-lord-in-residence defaulted on his mortgage and skipped town.

Decidia Skirball, whom I always will dislike intensely because of her hideous treatment of her brother, apparently decided to do something good for a change, and *she* bought Hobby Hills. All two hundred and twelve permanently overtaxed acres of it. Her plan was to divide 110 of those acres into large plots and sell them to rich expatriate New Yorkers like herself.

Fine. At worst, it will bring in much-needed tax revenues.

Fine. At best... it will still bring in much-needed tax revenues.

Other than buying Hobby Hills, the really good thing that she did was to deed over everything else, including the house, the barns, the stables, and Death Lake to her good-natured, freckle-faced son so that Andy could realize his dream of turning it into a summer camp for kids.

Andrew told me that he would ordinarily not have accepted such a big gift from his mother, fearing that it would come tied with a ribbon of interference and control. But from the moment he and Neverly presented Decidia with a granddaughter (named Morgana, in memory of his Uncle Morgan), his mother turned from a rapacious predator into a cooing dove.

Therefore, accepting the property had turned out to be plausible, possible, and practical.

As to Creedmore Snowdon, he experienced three devastating blows, one after the other. At least they would have been devastating to a normal human being. He, however, recovered from them so quickly that it confirmed a theory of mine that having neither character nor convictions can be a tremendous asset in certain people's lives.

The first blow was the birth of Andrew's daughter. The minute the child's grandmother took one look into Morgana's melty blue eyes, Creedmore was permanently evicted to a rarely visited back room in Decidia Skirball's heart.

Creedmore's second blow was losing his bid to become Killdeer's mayor.

I bet you're wondering how he managed to do *that*, since,

despite Herculean efforts on their parts, Sonny and Moe were not able to come up with a cure for being seventeen years old.

Those two irrepressible and unstoppable dynamos came up with a better scheme. They pooled their savings, including parts of their college education fund (a withdrawal they have thus far managed to hide from their parents), and the week before the election, they sent Boyd and Netty on a seven-day cruise, described by the boys as "an early anniversary present from your loving sons," to make sure that their father was safely out of town.

During that week, Sonny and Moe altered a few pronouns, forged a few signatures, scanned a few photographs, replaced a few dozen posters, and sent a revised press release to the local newspapers.

The objective of this frantic activity was to run their father for the office of mayor.

And guess what?

Boyd won!

Forty-two votes for him. Seven votes for Creedmore Snowdon.

Killdeer is not a big voting town.

When he came back from his vacation and discovered that he had unwittingly been elected the new mayor of Killdeer, Boyd's first inclination was to knock his two sons' heads together.

But Netty pointed out that the boys had merely taken it upon themselves to fight for principles in which they believed and that running their father for mayor had made them better citizens by involving them in the process of local government. Or at least, she was going to make that point, but she started laughing instead. And she couldn't stop. Then Boyd, observing Netty's uncontrollable hilarity, started to laugh himself.

Next thing you know, he was being sworn in as mayor.

The third blow from which Creedmore had absolutely no trouble recovering was the negative response that his television show received after he had aired a second segment about the Skirt Man's death and had announced that the producers of *Heaven and Earth* would contribute one hundred thousand dollars to the New York State Fire Academy for the scientific study of spontaneous human combustion and the greater understanding of its cause and effect.

That Vernon Roadigger was arrested for setting the fire that Creedmore was using as his trophy case did not faze him in the least. But then again, why would it? Facts were never a major obstacle to a man who believed in self-bending spoons, reincarnation, and ESP.

The New York State Fire Academy, by the way, accepted the TV show's donation with the caveat that *they* would be the ones who decided what educational purposes it would be used for.

To no one's surprise, the contribution was withdrawn.

We were equally unsurprised when Creedmore Snowdon sold his house in Killdeer and disappeared permanently from our lives.

And that pretty much sums it up. Except for a few minor things I think you will find of interest. Such as the disposition of the Skirt Man's property. Two weeks after he died, Daniel Bethlehem, an attorney from Norwich, notified all of the Skirt Man's beneficiaries that he was the executor of Morgan Mason's will. We then found out what Morgan had left and to whom.

Some of it was a shock.

Some of it was a blessing.

Some of it was out-and-out funny.

In the shock category, Sonny and Moe were left forty

acres each. Both parcels consisted of approximately one thousand feet of road frontage on Route 39 and each possessed a small trout creek.

In the blessing category, everything else that the Skirt Man had owned—including his house, his barn, his household furnishings, his books, his machinery, and his life savings—was left to "his best friend in the world," Lillian Roadigger.

Which only left the funny category. And what he did really *was* funny and gave just about everyone in town a well-deserved laugh. In his last bequest, Morgan Mason stated that he was leaving his satellite dish to Creedmore Snowdon, "who is obsessed with it and who is the biggest damn fool I ever met."

When Sonny and Moe heard about it, they slapped each other (and everybody else who got close) on the back, and hooted, "See. Didn't we tell you? We *told* you that Mr. Mason had a sense of humor!"

I don't know what I thought Lillian would do with the property she had inherited.

Sell it? Rent it? Raze it to the ground.

Surprisingly, she did the one thing that I had not even considered.

She decided to move in.

After I thought about it for about eight-tenths of a second, it made perfect sense. She had been happy there with him. He had been happy there with her. Maybe those memories would go a long way toward mending some of the broken places in Lillian's heart.

chapter 37

THE DAY AFTER Vernon Roadigger was arrested, my husband and brother decided to go back to the Skirt Man's house one last time.

"Why?" I asked.

We were in the kitchen, and Merry was still in bed. Or so I thought.

I had been uncharacteristically domestic that morning and had embellished the breakfast table with bowls of strawberries, slices of cantaloupe, cream cheese, lox, fresh bagels, and blueberry muffins.

Sebastian toyed idly with his butter knife.

Billy stared deeply into his coffee cup as if the coffee grounds at the bottom of the mug were capable of forecasting the future like tea leaves.

"Why do you want to go back?" I repeated, no longer thrilled by the idea of eating anything on that table myself.

"We're not sure," Sebastian said.

I turned to Billy.

He was still staring into his cup so I poked him in the arm.

He looked up and shrugged.

I placed my fork down on my plate and sighed.

"To hell with breakfast," I said. "Can I come, too?"

Sebastian reached over and squeezed my hand.

Billy smiled and winked.

They got up.

Apparently I had said the right thing.

I followed both men to the car.

Which is why I was with my husband and brother when they unlocked the Skirt Man's front door, poked through this room and that, rummaged through this drawer and that, and finally climbed the narrow flight of stairs.

It was upstairs that we found them.

They were lying at the bottom of a long-forgotten and dusty cigar box. The box itself was sitting on the narrow ledge of a small, rain-warped window in the Skirt Man's attic.

The air was still that Sunday morning. Still, quiet, and in some ways so daunting that we felt as if we had stepped into a museum diorama.

But Sebastian, who is either less sensitive to atmosphere than Billy and I, or more, reached over and tilted open the lid of the cigar box with a careful finger. We moved to either side of him, so mesmerized with anticipation that we did not hear the door to the house open and shut. And we did we not hear the footsteps on the stairs.

It wasn't until Sebastian removed a mottled sheet of folded paper from the box that we heard breathing and knew that somebody else was in the room.

I can't describe the shiver of fear I felt as my head snapped around. Or the exhalation of surprise and relief when my eyes beheld a tremulous Merry and the equally awed figures of Sonny and Moe standing at the very head of the stairs.

I knew why they were there.

They had come for the same reason that we had come.

They had come because something remained undone. None of us knew what it was, but whatever it was, we were going to do it.

I turned back to Sebastian.

He unfolded that aged and water-damaged sheet as gently and delicately as if he were unwrapping gauze around a package that contained the secret of life. While he was doing so, Billy reached into the cigar box.

He removed a small item that was attached to a white-bordered purple ribbon. It was a medal. In the center of the medal was the profile of George Washington.

Merry took a step forward.

"What is it?" she whispered.

Billy held it out. His voice was strangely soft as he said, "It's a Purple Heart."

"What—" Merry started to ask.

But Billy cut her off.

"The Purple Heart is a combat decoration given to members of the armed forces who were wounded in enemy action."

My daughter opened her hand.

Her uncle placed the medal into it. She examined it carefully and then passed it on to Sonny and Moe.

Billy continued to lift item after item out of the box. One by one we inspected them all: a Bronze Star, a Combat Infantry Badge, a Korean War Service Medal, a National Defense Medal, a United Nations Medal, an American Presidential Citation, a Korean War Commorative Medal. Each made its silent journey from hand to hand. We carefully noted the tiny

V on the ribbon of the Bronze Star, the open oval wreath and slender silver rifle on the Combat Infantry Badge, the embossed gold border surrounding an austere field of deepest blue on the Presidential Citation.

From what Lillian Roadigger had told us, we knew that Morgan Mason had been a Korean War veteran. Now we were learning the rest.

Learning being the operative word.

There was still so much left to discover. Still so many things that nobody in Killdeer knew. Still so much that even Lillian, who had loved him, had never been told.

The Skirt Man's secret lay hidden from view at the bottom of the old cigar box. It had become wedged underneath a fragment of paper lining that had come unglued. Billy gingerly raised the flap of paper, lifted it out, and balanced it between his thumb and forefinger.

Once again Merry whispered, "What is it?"

At first Billy did not answer. Nor did he look at Merry. He turned to Sebastian. Their eyes met. Then Billy looked away and started to speak. Or tried to. He had to stop for a moment to clear his throat. He closed his eyes. He opened his eyes. When words finally did come out, his voice was deep and hushed and reverential.

"This is the Congressional Medal of Honor." Again, he cleared his throat. "It is awarded to the bravest of the brave."

Merry extended her hand. Billy put the medal in her palm.

Six heads leaned forward.

We studied the five-pointed star, each point ending in an oak leaf. We studied the head of Minerva, goddess of wisdom and war. We studied the slim, fierce eagle that rested uneasily atop a gold bar inscribed VALOR.

"Turn it over," Moe said.

Merry gently rotated the medal in her hand.

She read aloud from the reverse side, "The Congress to Morgan Mason."

Then Sonny started to ask the question I had wanted to ask, but before he could get out the words, Sebastian, my dearest Sebastian, began to speak.

His eyes were narrowed and his head was bent intently over the barely legible piece of paper that he had found in the cigar box.

He read, with painstaking care, "*This Medal of Honor is awarded to*—I can't make out the next few sentences—*who distinguished himself conspicuously by valor and intrepidity at the risk of his life*—there's a water blot here—*observing his wounded comrades lying in an exposed position*—more water blots—*with incredible courage and stamina, he dauntlessly returned through withering fire and bursting shells and using only his rifle, he killed the entire enemy gun crew before falling unconscious from grenade and bullet wounds.* There are a few more sentences I can't read, but this part is clear—*the indomitable fighting spirit, extraordinary heroism, and tenacious devotion to duty clearly demonstrated by Cpl. Morgan Mason reflect the highest credit on himself, and uphold the honored traditions of...*"

Sebastian looked up.

"The rest is unreadable."

He turned to me, and for some reason I will never quite understand, my husband picked that moment for his eyes to bore into mine and his lips to silently form the words "I love you."

This time I was the one who had to close my eyes. I was the one who had to clear her throat.

Sebastian turned away.

Then, one by one, he replaced all of the medals in the cigar box.

Then carefully, he refolded that aged and fragile proclamation of unimaginably brave deeds.

Then meticulously and almost reluctantly, he repositioned the box on the narrow window ledge.

It was quiet up there in the attic as we stared at that cigar box.

We did not move.

The air did not move.

We barely breathed.

But we were terribly, terribly conscious of the man whose life had been so radically affected by the deeds for which he had been honored by the forgotten medals in that dusty box.

Then, without even glancing at each other, Sebastian and Billy suddenly stood at attention.

Merry, Sonny, Moe, and I instinctively followed suit.

And silently, without moving a muscle, we six who had come to know, honor, and respect Morgan Mason finally gave the Skirt Man his homecoming parade.

dedication

To the combat veterans in my life.

SAMUEL MOSES HURWITZ, Sergeant of the Canadian Grenadier Guards. The year my uncle Moe was drafted to play hockey for the Boston Bruins, he joined the army to fight Hitler instead. He was the most decorated noncommissioned officer in the Canadian Armoured Corps in World War II and was awarded the Distinguished Conduct Metal and the Military Metal. On October 23, 1944, the Guards, led by Sgt. Hurwitz's tank, were tasked with taking the village of Wousche-Plantage in Holland. His last radio message was "I am going forward, follow me when you can!" In the regimental newspaper, his troop commander wrote: "A little over a year ago, 23 Oct 1944 to be exact, this regiment lost one of its greatest men. A man whose character, leadership and personality were such that he will never be forgotten."

Every year, the Canadian Grenadier Guards Association presents the Hurwitz Cup to a young Army Cadet "in memory of one of the heroes of our regiment ... who is remembered by our veterans who fought in Europe as one of the finest members of our regiment."

DONALD FELDMAN served in the United States Army from August 18, 1948, to October 31, 1951. For his service in Korea, he was awarded the Combat Infantry Badge, the Bronze Star Medal with "V", the Purple Heart, and the Korean Service Medal with four bronze service stars. He is a full-time volunteer assisting other veterans at the Brooklyn VA Hospital. Donald was more than generous with his time and knowledge in helping me create Morgan Mason's service record during the Korean War.

BYRON HOUSTON COATES served sixteen years in the U.S. Marines, two of them as a gunnery sergeant. He was in Vietnam from 1969 to 1970. He was awarded the Combat Action Ribbon, the Vietnam Service Medal, the National Defense Service Medal, the Republic of Vietnam Cross of Gallantry (with palm), the Navy Achievement Medal (V), the Good Conduct Medal (Third Award), the Sea Service Ribbon, and the Rifle Expert Badge 8th Award. For the past seventeen years he has worked as a contractor for the Marine Corps pre-positioning ships and maintaining combat equipment. It was Byron, my brave and honorable friend, who introduced me to the George Orwell quotation: "People sleep peaceably in their beds at night only because rough men stand ready to do violence on their behalf."